Get Real

Also by Betty Hicks

Out of Order
Busted!
Animal House and Iz
I Smell Like Ham

Get Real

BETTY HICKS

A DEBORAH BRODIE BOOK
ROARING BROOK PRESS
NEW MILFORD, CONNECTICUT

A Deborah Brodie Book
Published by Roaring Brook Press
Roaring Brook Press is a division of
Holtzbrinck Publishing Holdings Limited Partnership
143 West Street, New Milford, Connecticut 06776

Library of Congress Cataloging-in-Publication Data
Hicks, Betty.
Get real / Betty Hicks.
p. cm.
"A Deborah Brodie book."
Summary: Destiny, a thirteen-year-old control freak who feels alienated in her
messy, haphazard family, helps her adopted best friend when she finds her birth
mother and decides to have a relationship with her. /6. 9 5
ISBN-13: 978-1-59643-089-1   ISBN-10: 1-59643-089-3
[1. Identity—Fiction. 2. Adoption—Fiction. 3. Friendship—Fiction. 4. Family
life—North Carolina—Fiction. 5. North Carolina—Fiction.] I. Title.
PZ7.H53155Ge 2006
[Fic]—dc22
2005028749

Roaring Brook Press books are available for special promotions and premiums.
For details, contact: Director of Special Markets, Holtzbrinck Publishers.

Book design by Jennifer Browne
Printed in the United States of America
First edition September 2006
2   4   6   8   10   9   7   5   3   1

ACKNOWLEDGMENTS

I owe my most heartfelt thanks to the many people who made valuable contributions to this book. To my editor, Deborah Brodie, for her always essential insight, expertise, and warmth.

To Betty Godwin at The Children's Home of North Carolina, for taking the time to educate me on North Carolina's adoption laws and practices. If there are any errors concerning adoption, they are mine and not hers. To Rebecca Conner, a former assistant public defender for juveniles, for verifying police procedures involving minors.

To Jennifer Browne, for her neat-child, messy-parents inspiration. To Lauren Wohl, for her words of wisdom and experience at the earliest and latest stages of this story. To Sandra Noelle Smith, for her expert error-spotting and helpful suggestions. To Tracey Adams, for being the best agent a writer could have. To Walt Sherlin, for obtaining the middle school information I needed. To Carol Taylor, for the "Moonlight Sonata" memory.

To Nate Conner, for fixing my computer each untimely time that it crashed. To Lise and David Sherlin, who inadvertently created the need for a Duke-Carolina game. To Will and Kim Hicks, without whom I would never have imagined a rare spotted newt. To Quinn Conner and Eli Hicks, who, just by being two and five, helped me create a very active three-year-old.

To Bill Hicks, for his unwavering confidence and support, even when the writing of this book took control of most of our summer vacation and all of my formerly stress-free disposition.

And to the knowledgeable and dedicated people at The Children's Home of North Carolina, who, sixty years ago, placed me with my "real" family.

❁

To the memory of my parents,
Nell and Nathan Ayers
And to my brother, Jere

❁

Chapter One

"Come on, Dez. You *have* to help me. We won't get caught."

It's night. Dark, rainy, and so cold that I can't understand why it isn't sleeting. The last thing I want to do right now—or ever—is steal a street sign.

"It's not even against the law," says Jil, her eyes pleading with me.

Not that I can see her eyes. Like I said—it's dark.

"Of course it's against the law," I screech. "Are you crazy?"

"They're widening this road soon," she answers in a firm, confident voice, the exact voice I imagine Christopher Columbus using to convince Queen Isabella that the world is round.

Jil's sure-about-everything voice has sucked me into more mistakes than a shark has teeth. It always begins with her saying, *Come on, Dez,* and ends with, *You have to help me.*

"They'll put up new signs," she continues with certainty. "We'll be doing the city a favor by taking this one away—one less chunk of metal to be hauled off to the dump."

I don't say anything, so she thumps the post with her fist and adds, "Do you know they charge by the pound to dump scrap like this in the city landfill? Taxpayers' money! I bet this sign is so heavy, we'll be saving—"

"Okay, okay," I interrupt, thinking, Maybe it's not stealing. At least not in a criminal way. I dig around in my coat pocket for a Kleenex. It's so cold, my nose is beginning to run.

All this trouble. Just because Jil's boyfriend's name is Graham, and she thinks he needs this particular green sign, with Graham Road in neat white block letters, for a Christmas present.

"I mean, what do you give somebody who has everything?" she had argued earlier, throwing up her hands in frustration.

"A street sign?" I'd asked doubtfully.

"Exactly," answered Jil.

I blow my nose and wonder what he'll give her. She pretty much has everything too. But where would Graham find a sign that says *Jil*? I mean, give me a break—one *L*? That's not how you spell it.

I wipe my nose again and wonder why cold weather always makes it drip. I should ask my mom, the scientist. She'd know.

What *I* know is that *Jil* should be spelled with two *L*s. As in *Jack and Jill*. Because she reminds me of a fairy-tale-type person. Okay, maybe *that* Jill is not actually in a fairy tale. She's a nursery-rhyme character, but hey, they're all related.

Anyway, the Jil who is standing here now—in the wet, freezing night—is just like the beautiful fairy-tale heroine, the one the bad guy always gives the *Do not* instructions to. You know. *Do not* set foot into that really tempting room with all the diamonds in it or a three-headed monster will eat you. Or *do not* take a single bite out of that juicy red apple or you'll fall asleep for a hundred years.

But Jil-with-one-*L* always does it anyway. And, big surprise, her three-headed monster inevitably turns into a gorgeous genie with six-pack abs, who grants her any three wishes she wants just because he thinks her energy and spunk are awesome.

That would be the same energy and spunk that, right now, is helping her jerk and shove a ten-foot-high signpost that's buried, solid, in deep dirt.

"Could you please help me here?" she begs, slightly out of breath.

I blow my nose again and scan the neighborhood for witnesses. Or police. An SUV swishes around the corner, its headlights exposing us for the criminals we're about to be. Two bright high beams pierce my eyeballs like sharp, cold knives.

"Stop pushing the sign!" I hiss.

Jil drops her hands and leans against the post, as if

we're just hanging out here for the sheer joy of it. Except that it's thirty-three degrees and raining.

The big vehicle swooshes past, spraying icy water up over the curb and onto my ratty, not-even-remotely-waterproof sneakers. Jil has on new, dry Gore-Tex boots.

I want to glare at her, but my eyes aren't up to it, and besides, she can't see them.

By now, the tissue I found in my pocket has soaked up all the runny nose it can hold, but I use it again anyway. Yuck. At least it beats using my sleeve.

Come on, Dez, I say to myself. Don't blame Jil. Didn't I sneak out here on my own two stupid, wet feet?

Come to think of it, I shouldn't criticize her name, either. With a name like Destiny, who am I to talk?

"You need a screwdriver," I say.

"What?"

"A screwdriver," I repeat. "You don't need the post. Just the sign."

Like I said, it's dark, so I can't see her eyes, but I know that they're blinking about a hundred miles an hour. Then they stop—I can feel it. A lightbulb moment.

"Dez!" she exclaims. Then she whacks her forehead, a dull thump that I assume is made with the palm of her hand, and says, "Duh. What would I do without you?"

Go to jail? I wonder.

Chapter Two

S tealing a street sign is not as easy as you might think.

Correction—*removing a no-longer-needed street sign* is not as easy as you might think.

First, we have to slog over to my house and find a screwdriver. Which is about as easy as locating a grape seed in a Dumpster full of garbage.

While Jil warms herself in front of a toasty fire, she chatters enthusiastically to my mother about the possibility of snow and school closings. Mom answers her with precise, expert commentary on barometric pressure, global warming, and the motion of molecules. My mother's favorite TV program is the Weather Channel. To Jil, this makes her interesting. To me, it makes her strange.

Meanwhile, I fumble my throbbing-and-thawing fingers through our rusty toolbox. My parents keep it in the hall closet, which is half filled with piles of my father's antique book collection of insanely old poetry. The toolbox has been shoved in the other half, under a stack of rectangular air filters that fit our old furnace—the one that died two years ago.

None of these disposable filters fit our new furnace, but my parents never throw anything away. Maybe they plan to use them as place mats.

The jumbled-up box is full of everything but tools: a wad of muddy string, a broken chain, one torn paperback book on how to identify trees in the winter—when the leaves are gone—a twisted tube of dried-up Super Glue, a toothbrush with no bristles, one faded red refrigerator magnet that used to say *Pizza Palace*, and a cockroach hotel with last century's expiration date on it.

And, *ick!* The smell! Musty books. Dead mice.

Mentally, I place the toolbox, and the closet, on my list of things to clean out. Also, to air out. Soon.

"Mom!" I shout. "Where's the screwdriver?"

No answer.

"Mom!"

"Hold your horses. I'm thinking."

Mom is a scientific genius, but—this is so weird—she says old-fashioned things all the time, like *hold your horses*. Sometimes I think she belongs back in the time of George Washington. Or Moses.

Maybe it's because she was raised by her grandmother. A perfectly normal sentence for Gram was "I'm tickled pink that you're as sharp as a tack, but don't bite the hand that feeds you, 'cause there's no such thing as a free lunch."

Clichés at my house are almost an art form.

"Why's Dez looking for a screwdriver?" I hear Mom ask.

Jil's Christopher Columbus voice answers. I can't make out exactly what she says, but the tone gets an A-plus in Convincing.

"Did you look in the bottom drawer in the kitchen?" Mom shouts back. "The one with the napkins?"

Why would I do that? I wonder. Then again, my house is the disorganized clutter capital of the universe, so why not look in the wrong place? Why not search the medicine cabinet or the sugar canister? Why not look up the chimney?

Jil and I trudge back out into the wet, icy night. Me carrying a screwdriver with a sticky, lint-covered handle that really was hidden in the napkin drawer—under a ceramic chicken and a six-year-old picture postcard from my great aunt in Salt Lake City.

Jil is tugging her left earlobe because that's what she does when she's nervous. Which makes me want to ask, if what we're about to do isn't stealing, then why are you acting twitchy? But I don't.

"Your mother said this will turn into snow," says Jil.

"Enough to close school?" I ask, hopeful.

"According to the weekend weatherman, one or two inches. According to your mom, at least four."

"*Wahoo!*" I cheer. In Durham, North Carolina, even a half inch is enough to call off school. I would love to have no class tomorrow. It's only December, but eighth grade is already old.

"What'd you tell Mom?"

"About what?"

"About why we need a screwdriver on a yucky Sunday night."

"Oh, I just said we were taking it to my house, so my mom could borrow it—that she couldn't find hers."

Jil and I both snort at the same time. What a joke!

Her mom's house would make the Library of Congress look disorganized. Everything in it is so neat, it wouldn't surprise me if she had ten screwdrivers, each lined up according to size, shape, and color, all in their very own drawer. Yellow plastic handles on the right, gray rubber handles on the left. None of them sticky.

Jil is so lucky.

I look up at the street sign. Way up. That's when I realize there's no chance that either of us can reach it.

"We need a ladder," says Jil, reading my mind.

"Right," I answer, "and a big megaphone to announce to every passing car that we're swiping a street sign."

"What we're doing is *not* the same as stealing!" Jil hisses at me. "Didn't I already explain?"

"Yeah, I know. We're doing the city a favor. But we're still going to look like crooks if we haul a ladder out here."

Jil and I both stare up at the tall sign. Tiny pellets of ice sting my face. The rain has changed to sleet.

"If I bend over, you can stand on my back," says Jil.

I think about that solution for all of two seconds. I'm bigger than Jil. Not fat, but solid. Five feet, eight inches. Jil is barely five feet, and thin, like the post we're gaping up at, only with curves. My mom thinks she's *as cute as a button*. Boys think so, too.

What boys think about me—if they think about me—is that I'm taller than they are.

If anybody stands on anybody, I'm going to be the one stuck on the bottom. Me—Dez. The pillar. Sturdy. And sometimes stupid.

I bend over. "Climb on up."

"Are you *sure*?" asks Jil.

"Just do it," I groan, even though I'm pretty positive that I don't want her Gore-Tex boots grinding into my back. My quilted nylon jacket is water resistant, not water-proof, and I'm already half soaked.

Jil's coat is made of warm down, 100 percent water-proof, Patagonia's finest Arctic-expedition weight. She could camp out here until spring and never feel a chill.

"Thanks, Dez," she says, scrambling up onto my hunched-over back, then pulling herself up straight with the signpost. "You're the best."

"No kidding," I mutter back.

We both giggle.

Even when we're both stupid and miserable, Jil is my best friend, and I am hers.

I try to keep myself level by placing my hands on my legs, elbows slightly bent, and pushing hard against my thighs.

Jil's a lot heavier than she looks.

"Stand still!" I hiss.

"Sorry."

Now she's pinching the skin around my shoulder blades with her complicated boot treads. Sleet is pelting against the back of my neck, slipping down, and melting under my sweater.

"What're you doing?" I scream.

"I can't reach it," she whimpers.

"Stretch!" I yell. I feel her boots pinch the skin around the top of my spine, and wonder if she will sever all my nerve endings and paralyze me for life.

An icy gust of wind whips through every layer of clothing I'm wearing. I might as well be naked.

"The screwdriver!" she shouts. "It won't work. There's no slot—"

"Car!" I yell, standing up straight.

Jil crashes to the ground beside me. I lose my footing and fall on top of her. Something rips. A low, dark sports car streaks by—a piercing missile of light that vanishes into the darkness.

Jil doesn't move.

"Are you all right?" I ask, rolling off her, panicked.

No answer. Then I hear her groan and slowly push herself into a sitting position. She's rubbing her head.

"Fool!" She spits the word into the night.

"I'm so sorry," I apologize.

"Not *you*," she moans. "That moron going sixty on an icy road. I hope he gets a ticket."

I laugh, relieved.

"A wallet," she says, out of nowhere.

"A wallet?"

"Yeah," she says. "Graham is getting a wallet for Christmas."

We sit under the street sign and laugh hysterically as the stinging sleet turns into tiny flecks of soft snow. I pat my hands over my jeans, searching for what tore, but everything seems to be in one piece.

I'm so cold, though, that I'm numb all over, except for my back. It still hurts where Jil clogged across it. But weirdly, I'm happy to be sitting here in a freezing, wet heap with her, watching the snow fall.

Somehow, even though snow is just as cold as sleet—and colder than freezing rain—it feels better. Cozier.

"It's beautiful," says Jil.

I purr a little *umm* of agreement, and open my mouth to catch the quiet flakes on my tongue.

We're both silent for a long time. I'm thinking how amazing snow is. Wishing Durham got more than two or three decent accumulations every year. Listening for the occasional *ticks* of sleet mixed in. Hoping for no school tomorrow.

I wonder what Jil is thinking.

"Dez," she says, so softly I have to lean closer to hear, "there's something really important I have to do."

Uh-oh. It's her so-solemn-that-it's-scary voice. I bet she's pulling on her earlobe. Any second now she'll say, *Dez. You have to help me.*

This calls for an instant subject change. "So," I blurt, "what time is it?"

Jil pushes the button that lights her watch and squeals,

"Oh my God! I'm late!" She hops up, brushes snow off her pants, and says, "Gotta go. I'll call you tomorrow!"

I watch her sprint for home, her surprised shriek still echoing in my ears. But deeper inside my head, I hear the other voice, the one that was as serious as a cemetery. The one that said, *Dez. There's something really important I have to do.*

Chapter Three

B efore I went to sleep, I set my alarm clock for six A.M., in case of snow.

Dad'll wake up early too. Without turning on a single light in his bedroom, he'll click on the TV. *Ping!* Even from my room across the hall, I'll hear it pop on with that little electronic twang. He'll lie there half-asleep, scratching his bristly red beard and watching to see if Carrington Middle School scrolls across the bottom of a screen that's glowing spooky blue in the early-morning dark.

If he sees my school, he'll nudge Mom; then they'll both sit up and watch the day-care closings. If La Petite Academy shows up, I'll hear their low planning voices, deciding whose schedule can best be rearranged to stay home with Denver, my little brother.

But I'm awake this early for a different reason. A reason so secret that I would never even tell Jil, because best friend or not, she would think it is way too weird.

I am awake to see the snow.

Not to see *if* it snowed. And not to let out a tiny

whoop, yawn, and crash back into bed to sleep late—like normal thirteen-year-old girls do.

No. I set my alarm clock so I can see the snow before anyone else does. To see the downy cover that drifts over my front yard and actually lights up the darkness with its smooth white shine. I want to see it before Denver plows into it and fills it full of footprints and snow angels. And ruins it.

I want to see it neat.

The way I keep my room.

Sometimes I wonder how I can even be related to Mom, Dad, and Denver. The three most un-neat people in the history of the world.

Slobs.

Don't get me wrong. I love my brother.

And for parents, mine are okay.

But . . . sooo embarrassing.

I pull the cord slowly to open my curtains. My room has a picture window that takes up most of one wall and looks out onto our front yard. To me, it's a real drum-roll moment, like when the curtains part at the beginning of a play and there's a whole new world hidden behind them. A room filled with soft, rich, velvet furniture, smelling of pipe tobacco. Or a big city square crowded with old-timey streetlights and boys in knickers waving newspapers and shouting, "Extra! Extra! Read all about it!"

I smile at the scene opening outside my window.

Snow.

Clean. White. The ground completely covered. At least four inches worth. The bushes have huge cotton-ball clumps on top. And best of all, there's a flat river of ice-milk where the street should be.

No school. For sure.

I climb back into bed, hug my knees to my chest, and look out at how perfect it all is. I figure I have at least thirty minutes before Mom grabs a broom and whacks all the snow off the bushes, so the weight of it won't bend and break the branches of her boxwoods.

I wonder if I'll need to babysit. Mom and Dad would never make me watch Denver all day, because I can't. *Like a tiger in your tank*, says Mom. Or, *if he were any busier, he'd be twins*.

Nobody, except parents or experienced professionals, can handle Denver all day.

But they might need me for an hour or two. Dad teaches Eighteenth-Century Lit and Epic Poetry at Duke. Between classes he shuts himself inside his campus office, surrounded by a million little scraps of scribbled-on white paper, and translates poetry from Latin or Greek or Gaelic or something. He turns it into English that still doesn't make sense.

Mom's an environmental scientist who does a bunch of different things. Some days she wears steel-toed boots and a hard hat and runs groundwater pump tests. Other days she puts on nice clothes and meets with developers and industries. Her favorite job is wading around in rubber boots doing what she calls pond research. I call it pond slime–search.

Anything outdoors makes her happy. Since it snowed, though, she probably won't work outside, and she may have to put on her good clothes, look professional, and meet with money-crazy clients. That's the part of her job she hates.

I watch the whiteness glow even whiter as it slowly gets lighter outside, and hope that I can spend most of my day at Jil's house. She lives three streets over. No distance at all if I cut through two backyards. But because of the snow, I'll stick to the streets. I hate messing up someone else's smooth yard as much as I hate it when Denver wrecks my own.

Jil's house is amazing. It's three times bigger than mine and has a basement with a pool table, a zillion video games, and a refrigerator full of Dr. Pepper, Mountain Dew, root beer, Evian—you name it. It also has built-in stereo speakers, a giant plasma TV screen, and more DVDs than I can count. In the living room, there's a black grand piano so shiny that I can see my face in it.

But those aren't the main reasons I hang out there. Honest.

I hang out there because I love how neat it is. Everything in order. Or filed away. Labeled. And because my house gives me a headache.

I wait until I think Jil's got to be awake—around ten o'clock—and then I call her. Denver has been up long enough to watch one episode of *Dragon Tales*, two *Blue's*

Clues videos, and turn our beautiful front yard into a crime scene of snow abuse.

Mom has run four dryer loads of the same wet snow-suit, made two batches of snow cream, and heated up one monster pot of hot chocolate.

Denver is small, but major.

Jil answers her phone on the fourth ring.

"You awake?" I ask.

"Yeah," she lies.

"Get up!" I yell.

"Okay. Okay. Okay. Hold your horses."

"You sound like my mother."

"I like your mother," she mumbles sleepily.

"Me too," I say. "Sometimes."

I mean, what's not to like? If only she weren't so messy and so . . . so . . . I have to search for a word to describe my mother. *Blah*, I think. That's it! She's just so *blah*.

"Now, get up!" I shout at Jil.

"You want to come over?"

"Yes."

"When?"

"Now."

I click off the phone and grab my coat, which is still damp from last night. Dad has morning classes, so he's gone, but he'll be back by one o'clock. Mom has to leave by noon to meet a client. That means I have Denver-duty for the lunch hour in between—which gives me two whole hours at Jil's house.

"Isn't it beautiful?" says Mrs. Lewis, opening the front

door after I ring the bell. "But so cold." She hugs herself and shivers, her laugh soft and welcoming, like music. "Quick, come inside." She touches my sleeve, then tugs me into the warm house.

"Yes." I totally agree. The snow is beautiful. But so is she. Smiling, friendly, and looking perfect, even in a bathrobe, fluffy slippers, and zero makeup.

"Snow day," she explains, sweeping her hand over her not-dressed self. She points to the stairs and adds, "Jil's upstairs."

I hurry up the stairs, straight to Jil's room. For an hour, I watch her brush her teeth, comb her hair, make her bed, and eat a bowl of Rice Krispies with big, juicy red strawberries sliced all over it. Then she has an English muffin spread with homemade fig jam. Her refrigerator is always filled with colorful ripe fruit, even in winter. Her pantry shelves look like a magazine ad for healthy living.

The food at *my* house looks like the packaged stuff that comes in cheap gift baskets. No kidding. Moldy beef sticks, imitation garlic cheese spread, and tiny little sample jars of orange marmalade.

I hate orange marmalade. If you ask me, it tastes like barely sweetened ear wax.

"Let's play 'Chopsticks,'" I beg.

Lately, I have fallen in love with the piano at Jil's house. We play duets on it. Easy, kid ones like "Chopsticks." But I want to learn a real song. Something serious and symphonic that will convince my parents that I deserve a piano. And lessons.

"Money doesn't grow on trees," says Mom.

"Remember the violin," says Dad.

In fourth grade, I begged them to buy me a violin and swore that I would play it forever. That I would practice every day. That someday, I would sit in the first chair for the New York Philharmonic.

And I might have, too. But nobody had clued me in about how violins work. You have to push one set of fingers down on the strings while the other hand slides a long bow back and forth over the strings, pulling notes out.

But they're not precise notes. Because there is no guide, or button, or ivory key that tells you the exact spot that will produce a B-flat or an A. Your fingers just have to know that somewhere on that long string, between some lines that are way too far apart to help, is an E, or an F-sharp.

My fingers never knew how to find such demanding places. One day I could put my finger high up on the second string and get a good sound. The next day, out would squeak some off-key note that wasn't right at all. The whole thing seemed messy to me.

But a piano! Each white key, each black key—an exact note. No guesswork. All I have to do is hit the ivory rectangle to the left of the two black keys, and out comes the most perfect C you ever heard.

A piano is precise. Neat. Everything in its place. Every day.

Jil pulls up the bench and begins to play a stream of beautiful notes.

"You've been practicing."

She shrugs. "Some."

It's so unfair. I would kill to have a piano and lessons, and Jil could care less about it. What really slays me is that Jil is adopted, which means that she totally *lucked* into this awesome house and family.

"What is that?" I whisper.

The sound flows out from her fingers, a smooth river of notes, ascending, repeating, over and over. Then, lower. Suddenly punctuated by a bright splash of new sound. Higher.

Just like the smooth expanses of snow rolling across the lawns that I saw on my way over here. I'd spotted a bright red cardinal landing in a tree, a sudden fluttering flag of amazing color against the smooth, clean white.

The music sounded just like that had looked, surprising my heart and making it swell up the exact same way.

"'Moonlight Sonata,'" Jil answers.

"Teach me."

"Sure." Abruptly, she stops playing.

I put my left hand where she tells me. Then I hit three notes. Pinky, to middle finger, to thumb. Ascending. *Tah-dah-dah. Tah-dah-dah. Tah-dah-dah.*

I sound almost like Jil! Cool! This is easy.

"Okay," I say, excited. "Now, show me the right hand."

This part is harder. I can't make the happy splash of sound come in at the right time, so I go back to practicing the low, smooth *tah-dah-dah*s that my left hand is loving.

"Dez," says Jil.

"Yeah?" I answer, happily *tah-dah-dah*ing.

"There's something really important I have to do," she says.

Plink-plunk-plunk. My fingers lose their rhythm.

Not now, I think. I pretend I don't hear her, and try to find the right notes again.

Tah-dah-dah. Tah-dah-dah. Yes!

"Dez," she says louder. "Listen to me. Please."

I rest my hands on the keyboard. Trying to hold my place. Hoping I'll get to come back. I can't remember the last time anything felt so perfect to me.

I turn my head toward Jil, sitting beside me, looking weird. Pulling her earlobe.

"You know I'm adopted. Right?"

"Of course I know you're adopted," I say. But my brain is spinning into the far reaches of the stratosphere, trying to grasp what that could possibly have to do with me learning to play her piano.

As it turns out, it has nothing whatsoever to do with it, because the next thing she says is, "I've decided to find my birth mother."

"Your what?" I drop my hands from the keys and twist my whole body to face her.

"My birth mother. You know. My *real* mother. The-one-who-actually-gave-birth-to-me-but-didn't-keep-me."

The last part spills out of Jil's mouth like a thumb racing across the piano keys in one long, fast, jarring note. Her face is flushed a hot, sweaty pink.

I stare.

"And Dez," she whispers. "You *have* to help me."

Chapter Four

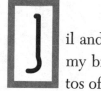il and I are back at my house, ready to babysit my brother. Mom is lecturing me on the how-tos of Denver-duty.

1. How to get Denver to eat if he doesn't want to.
2. How to get Denver to nap if he doesn't want to.
3. How to get Denver to breathe if he doesn't want to.

"Mother," I say. "It's only for one hour. I can do this."

"His blinkie's in the dryer," she continues. "Make sure he washes his hands. Don't cut his sandwich in half or he won't eat it."

"Mom!"

"I just want to make sure—"

"Go!" I say. "You'll be late for your meeting."

She rolls her eyes and adjusts the blouse under her suit jacket so that the collar comes out over the lapels. I'd bet anything that shirt still has yesterday's mustard stain on it, and that she's covered it up by buttoning her jacket. My mom, the scientist, whose clients think she's neat, tall, smart, and professional.

Well, she is smart, professional, and tall. But neat ha! She's never worn anything neat in her life, except to meetings, because she has to. Her home and every-where-else uniform is gloomy gray sweats in the winter, and ankle-length cotton shifts with no waist in the sum-mer. Accessorized with clunky tennis shoes and a fanny pack slung low on one hip. She looks like a tourist.

Comfort is the fashion creed at my house.

The way I see it, Mom and Dad were born at the wrong time. They should definitely have grown up in the sixties, when they would've had so many more cre-ative outlets for their hippie genes. They were totally made for flower power, war protests, and living in com-munes.

Instead, they were teenagers in the eighties, when the best they could do was follow The Dead. The Grateful Dead, that is. That's how they met. Love at first sight, over a VW bus. My mom spotting my dad, a body-pierced soul mate selling green-and-yellow tie-dyed T-shirts.

And then there's the part that came later, when they got married and named their kids Destiny and Denver.

If I could've had my choice, would I rather have been tagged with a town in Colorado, or the touchy-feely drama-noun that I got stuck with?

I don't know.

Either way, it's embarrassing.

Did I mention that my father wears shirts that look like pajama tops and quotes poetry in the middle of conversations?

Which is why I don't understand Jil at all. She has an incredible mom, an incredible dad, an incredible everything. And now she wants to go round up some woman who is a total stranger so that she can have . . . have what? Two mothers? A spare? Just the new mom? Can I have her old mom?

As the kitchen door closes behind my mother, I pick up a sponge that looks as if it cleaned up World War I and toss it into our garbage can. I open a new pack and wipe the kitchen counter where Mom spilled jelly while she was starting to make Denver's sandwich.

"Jil," I say as I pull out a clean knife and spread peanut butter on a piece of bread, "why do you want another mom?"

"It's on the wrong half," says Denver.

Huh?

I look down at the slice of white bread on the counter. The one I just spread with peanut butter. The piece next to it, the one that Mom prepared, is covered with grape jelly.

"The jelly goes on the other one."

"It's important," says Jil.

"That the jelly goes on the other one?!" I exclaim.

"No," she says. "That I find my mom."

"Oh." I slap the two halves together.

"Don't cut it!" yells Denver.

"Don't worry," I tell him, plopping the sandwich on a chipped plate and sliding it across the island to where Denver sits perched at the bar counter, his feet dangling two feet off the floor. He's still wearing his snow boots, and there's a puddle of water where the ice he dragged in has melted onto our scarred fake-tile floor.

"I thought there was a law," I say to Jil. "I thought you couldn't find out the identity of your birth parents until you're eighteen."

"What are birth parents?" asks Denver, staring suspiciously at his sandwich as if he's trying to decide if his tongue will fall off if he eats it with the peanut butter on the wrong side.

Jil makes a zip-it motion across her lips and glares at me.

"Eat your lunch," I tell Denver. Then I reach across and flip his sandwich over. "See?" I say. "I fixed it."

He picks up the sandwich and looks underneath. Then he takes a tiny bite. What Mom doesn't know is that I can make Denver do things he doesn't want to without all her tricks. I have my own tricks. But my best one is not putting up with his weirdness.

I pour apple juice into a bright green sippy cup and set it down beside his plate. "Let's go in the den." I motion Jil to follow.

"You can't leaf me," Denver complains.

"I'm not leaving you. I'm just going in the other room. So you can prove to me what a big boy you are."

Then, for his dining entertainment, I pop a Disney song disc into his blue plastic player.

"'Kay," he answers happily, taking a bigger bite of his sandwich.

"She called my house," says Jil as soon as we get out of earshot of bigmouth boy. Denver has a bad habit of repeating things he's not supposed to know.

"*Who* called your house?"

"My real mother."

"You mean, your birth mother."

"Same thing."

I gape at Jil. I'm not so sure it is the same thing.

Jil sits down on our sofa and looks up at me. Expectantly. Excitedly.

I slump onto the seat of Dad's recliner, careful to keep it upright. Crinkly bulges greet my butt. I lean forward slightly and sweep the lumpy pile of magazines and weeks-old newspapers to the floor.

"I heard them talking on the phone," says Jil. "Mom and my real mom. Only I didn't know it was her until later."

Jil is sitting on the edge of our couch, leaning forward and moving her hands as if she's telling a ghost story.

"I heard Mom saying stuff like 'But we agreed. No contact until Jil is older,' and 'I'll send more pictures. Please. Don't call here again.' When she hung up, I asked her who it was, and she said, 'Wrong number,' with her face all red and splotchy-looking. Then she flew straight up the stairs to where my dad was reading in their bedroom, and slammed the door."

Wow. I couldn't imagine Mrs. Lewis slamming anything. "You listened," I state.

"Of course I listened. Mom told Dad, 'Jil's mother called again.' She said it as if she'd called before. And her voice was all quivery, like she was about to cry."

No kidding, I think, imagining what a colossal surprise all this would be to Mrs. Lewis. Mr. Lewis. And to Jil. I stare at the messy pile of papers I'd dumped on the floor and try to imagine how upset all of them must be. I also think about how every one of these old newspapers should have been thrown away a week ago.

"Then they said a bunch of legal stuff that I didn't totally get," Jil continues. "But here's the deal. I know I have something called an independent adoption. Mom and Dad told me that a million years ago. It means they actually met my mom. Briefly. She was a friend of our next-door neighbor's cousin's girlfriend, or something like that. They arranged my adoption through a lawyer, not an agency, because agencies take forever and they wanted a baby so much. Right away."

"They know your mother?" I look up, stunned.

"Yeah," says Jil, her eyes locked onto mine. "They even send her pictures of me, at least once a year, with a letter telling her stuff I'm doing, like tying my shoes or learning to ride a bike. But—no contact."

"*No contact*," I echo. "I always thought, with adoptions, nobody knew anybody, forever."

"Most adoptions," says Jil. "Nobody knows anybody. Forever. Or, sometimes, until you're at least eighteen and really want to know. But mine's different."

Jil sits straighter. She clenches her fists in front of her heart. "She wants to meet me. I just know it."

If eye expressions could burn, hers would burst into flames. "Dez," she says, "I want to meet her, too."

Oh, no. That sounds like a mistake to me, but I've seen that look before. Like the time she decided she wanted to learn to play tennis and nine months later she won the club championship for her age group.

My head is swimming with questions and doubts. I stare down at the paper pile and try to straighten it a little with my feet.

"Stop cleaning up!" snaps Jil.

"Sorry." I jump as if I've been caught cheating on a test. I know I can be a little nutty about my neatness thing. Sometimes it's a curse.

"But your mom told her not to call anymore. Right?"

"Right." The energy pulsing out of Jil's eyes right now could launch a rocket ship to the moon.

"So, that's the end of it. Right?"

"It's broke!" Denver whines from the kitchen. He marches into the room holding out his toy disc player, which appears to be pretty much swimming in grape jelly. His hair is filled with peanut butter. And his fingers are a combination of both.

"Noooo," I groan, snatching up the player before it oozes permanent purple onto the carpet. I head for the kitchen sink. As I wipe away the mess, I wonder if Mom and Dad will make me pay to replace it.

"Wrong," says Jil, her eyes narrowing to two tiny slits.

"He's only three," I answer.

"No, I mean you're wrong about this being the end of it."

"End of what?" says Denver.

"None of your business," I growl, peeling off a paper towel and pushing it into the tiny speakers with a clean knife blade.

"But, what can you do?" I ask Jil.

She sticks out her right thumb and pinky and holds them up to her ear, like a telephone.

Denver does the same thing with his PB&J hand.

"No way," I say. "You don't know her name or number."

"Whose name or number?" asks Denver.

Jil points to our phone.

"Telephone," says Denver, picking up the kitchen phone with his gooey purple and peanutty fingers and saying, "Hello. Denver's res-dence."

Jil pries the now-yucky phone away from him. She dangles it with two fingers to minimize her contact with its freshly-coated peanut butter and jelly finish, and points to the small clear screen above the numbers.

"What?" I say, wishing we could just talk. Wishing we didn't have to dream up sign language to fool Denver. And hoping this disc player will play again when I finish scooping jelly out of it.

And then I get it.

Of course.

Jil's mother's number is saved on the Lewises' Caller ID.

Chapter Five

I don't understand Jil.

Not at all.

I gape at her while she grins expectantly at me, still pointing to the Caller ID window on my telephone. Would she really have the nerve to call up her long-lost mother? The one who's a total I-know-zero-about-you stranger?

Would meeting her be exciting, or creepy?

Brave, or dumb?

Would it make Jil's parents mad, or sad?

"Wh-what the heck will you say?" I stammer. "'Hey, you don't know me?'" I toss the paper towel that's all icky with peanut butter and jelly into our trash can. "How about, 'Hello, we met in the delivery room a long time ago, but you might not recognize me anymore because the brown birth hair that I had fell out and came back blond?'"

Jil's eyes burn into mine. "Dez," she shouts. "This is *not* funny!"

Of course it's not funny. It's scary. That's why I tried to make a joke.

Blap! A car door slams shut in our driveway.

"Daddy!" screams Denver, running as fast as his tiny, snow-booted feet will carry him. He reaches up, turns the handle, and flings open the back door just in time for Dad to stomp through. He's wearing an old canvas parka with an ugly plaid scarf wrapped around his neck. His funny, flat wool cap is flecked with snow. Dad says it's called a driver's cap, but lots of people drive, and Dad is the only person I've ever seen wearing a hat like this. It looks sort of like a beret but with a brim in front.

He stuffs his cigarette out in the ashtray that I keep just inside the door. It's there because I finally convinced him that I would die an early death from secondhand smoke if he puffed away in every room in the house. I try not to think about *his* early death.

He still smokes in his home office, though—the room right off our den that always smells like burned dirt.

Dad's tall and thin, with very pale skin and a red beard that covers his face like a worn-out scrub brush—short wiry bristles everywhere. It makes him look Scottish, but he's not.

"Ah," exclaims Dad, "my *swift runner Achilles!*" He sweeps Denver up into his arms and hugs him.

"No, Daddy," says my brother, giggling. "I'm Denver."

"And," continues Dad, smiling warmly at Jil, *"fair Helen—the face that launched a thousand ships."*

See what I mean? Who talks like that?

Nobody.

Except my dad. He teaches poetry. He translates

poetry. And every chance he gets, he speaks poetry. *Old* poetry. Just like a foreign language.

Achilles, pronounced *Uh-kill-ees* in case anyone wants to know, is the hero that Brad Pitt plays in the movie *Troy*. And Helen is a woman so beautiful that a thousand ships got launched and a million guys jumped on board just so they could sail off somewhere and die trying to rescue her.

Dad did not see the movie. And he won't. He gets all his information straight from Homer. Not Homer Simpson. There is a less famous Homer who lived a very long time ago and wrote a thousand-page epic that Dad apparently memorized. It's called *The Iliad*, but I don't know why, because none of the characters are named that.

Jil's face is flashing splotches of red. Is that because Dad just compared her to one of the most gorgeous women who ever lived? Or because she's still mad at me for making fun of finding her mother?

I wasn't making fun. Not really. I wouldn't do that. I'm just nervous about what's going to happen next.

Dad lowers Denver to the floor, then stamps snow off his favorite shoes—Hush Puppies. The fakey suede is stained dark where they've completely soaked through. Who wears Hush Puppies in the snow? Who wears Hush Puppies, period?

Dad leans over and kisses me on the top of my head. "And how's my—"

"Not now, Dad." I cut him off before he can call me his "fair nymph" or "fairy queen."

"My player's busted," whines Denver.

"I'd better go now," says Jil.

"Me too," I add.

"Wait," Dad says. "Not so fast. What's wrong with Denver's toy? It looks fine to me."

"That's because I fixed it." I want to add that, also thanks to me, the kitchen counter is clean and the den carpet is free of grape jelly, but who would care?

I pop the Disney disc back into the plastic player and hope that it really is fixed. The opening *um-deedle-deedle-deedle* notes of "Supercalifragilisticexpialidocious" fill the kitchen.

"Thanks, Dez!" shouts Denver.

Dad frowns. He's not an *um-deedle-deedle-deedle* Supercalifragilisticexpialidocious kind of guy. But he can't figure out how to keep well-meaning relatives from giving us toys that aren't hand carved out of sacred wood by wise and ancient tribespeople.

"Let's read," Dad suggests, pushing down the *off* button.

Denver follows him happily into the den. He insists that he actually loves it when Dad reads old and boring stuff out loud to him. Personally, I think he just likes sitting on Dad's lap so he can push his baby thumbs into Dad's prickly red beard.

I grab my coat and scoot out the back door with Jil.

"Be home '*ere the setting sun*,'" calls Dad.

"You bet," I shout back.

"Your dad is so cool," says Jil.

I shoot her a *Yeah, right* look.

"No, I mean it."

"Are you really going to call your birth mother?" I ask.

"Yes," she whispers, so quietly I almost don't hear it over the crunching of our feet on the snow-crusted ruts in our driveway.

"When?" I ask.

"Now," Jil answers, only slightly louder.

I watch the word come out of her mouth in a small, round puff of cold white breath. For one whole second, it hangs in the air where, I swear, I can see it. Then it's gone. But it leaves behind a killer vibration that makes my stomach lurch, exactly the way it did one day last month when I saw Denver reach, on tiptoe, into a kitchen drawer and pull out a carving knife.

I plod with Jil toward her house, walking as slowly as I possibly can. I need time to decide if I should try and talk her out of calling her birth mom.

Half the neighborhood yards are trashed where kids have played, destroying all the smooth white covers of snow. Ugly faded grass shows through where almost every flake in the Muncys' front yard has been rolled into balls for making snow people. Seven of them. All wearing funny hats. Plus one bumpy mound that looks as if it is supposed to be a turtle. Or a football.

The sun has melted some of the snow, but enough will refreeze tonight to make the roads way too dangerous for school.

Yay!

And everybody's yard will form a hard crust that, if

you jump on it, will break and stick up like huge pieces of broken glass.

Why do I feel like that's exactly what Jil is about to do? To jump on a big plate-glass window and break it into a hundred daggers, points up.

The smell of warm chocolate smacks both of us in the face as soon as we open Jil's front door. In her so-clean-it-squeaks kitchen, Mrs. Lewis has spread freshly baked chocolate chip cookies on a beautiful platter. Next to it are pear-shaped white dessert plates, draped with red-and-white checked napkins made out of real cloth.

"Hungry?" She smiles at us, looking like a model for a fitness ad. She and Mr. Lewis play tennis so much, they have tans all year.

She's daintily eating something white and soft out of a small crystal bowl. "Want some?" she asks.

"What is it?"

"Curds and whey," she answers.

"Nuh-uh," says Jil, rolling her eyes. "It's yogurt."

"Same thing," says her mom, winking in my direction.

"Really!" I exclaim. "Curds and whey is yogurt? Little Miss Muffet was eating *yogurt*!?"

"Um-hmm." Mrs. Lewis nods as she glides another vanilla spoonful gracefully into her mouth.

"Honest?"

"Honest."

I am so amazed. Now *that* is useful literary information. Way better than somebody's face launching a thousand ships.

Jil and I pile two plates with cookies. I thank Mrs. Lewis.

"Your mother is so cool," I say as soon as we're out of the kitchen.

Jil shoots me a *Yeah, right* look.

"No, I mean it," I say, spraying a few cookie crumbs out of my mouth. I bend over to pick them up off the shiny hardwood floor.

"Don't bother," says Jil. "Mom vacuums three times a day."

Even I know that's an exaggeration, so I ignore Jil, pick up the cookie pieces anyway, and head for the living room. And the piano. I can't wait to play it again.

"Not now." Jil steers me away from the shiny black piano and up the stairs to her room—the room that has been decorated with a poppy-patterned fabric in tangerine and fuchsia on a white background. Cool throw pillows that look like flowers coordinate the look, along with striped fabric that makes it all magically come together. All created by some amazing new Japanese designer whose name I can't remember.

Who knew that stripes went with flower patterns? The ones at my house don't. Neither do the ugly plaids.

Jil, still chewing her last cookie bite, picks up her cell phone and starts to punch in numbers.

"Now?" I shriek. "You're calling her now?"

"Got to," she says. "Or I'll lose my nerve."

I dive across her bed and grab the phone.

"Hey!" Jil snatches it back.

"Please," I say. "Think about this. Have you talked to your parents?"

"No."

"Are you going to?"

"No."

"Why not?"

"Because they might not let me do it," she says defensively. Then she swallows, lowers her face so I can't see it, and adds, "and because it might hurt their feelings."

"Well, *yeah!*" I say, way too loud.

Jil starts punching numbers again.

I watch, my eyes glued to her as though I'm watching an action movie—one where I know something colossal is about to happen, but I don't know if it'll be bad or good.

"Hello," says Jil, sounding way calmer than she looks. She's stretching her earlobe a mile—as if it's made of taffy. "May I speak to . . . uh . . . I mean . . . are you . . . ?"

She stops.

Oh, no! Jil doesn't even know her name.

Her red face-splotches pop back out like instant hives.

Jil's left hand, the one that was pulling her ear, is squeezed into a white-knuckled knot. Her right, the one that's gripping her cell phone, is trembling.

"This is Jil," she says into the telephone. "Are you my mom?"

Chapter Six

Jil's face blotches glow, so inflamed it wouldn't surprise me if, any minute, they catch her cell phone on fire.

After asking, "Are you my mom?" Jil has said "yes" twice and "no" three times. I counted.

The rest of the time she's just listened. I've twisted my shirt into one gigantic knot, so scrunched up that the wrinkles will never come out.

What's her mom saying? What's Jil thinking? Why doesn't she talk? Or smile? Or cry? Why doesn't she hang up and tell me what's happening, for Pete's sake?

"Yes," says Jil. That's yes number three. But this one's different. This one has a smile with it—a tiny smile. It looks like the kind that feels big on the inside, but that you try to hold back on the outside.

"I'd like that," Jil whispers into the phone. "Very much." Bigger smile. "Can I bring a friend?"

"What!" I screech.

Jil glares at me while jerking her index finger up to her lips.

Guiltily, I clap my hand over my mouth.

Jil scribbles something on a notepad, then clicks off her phone. Gently, she folds it closed. Her mouth spreads into a huge grin that lasts about two seconds before it contorts into a puckered mess, and tears stream down her face.

I rush to hug her. "It's okay," I say, wrapping my arms around her. "Whatever she said, it's okay."

"No, no," she says, pushing me back gently. "It's good. It's all good. Honest."

She's smiling again, but she's still crying, all at the same time. Kind of like a rainbow in a drizzle.

I back off, plopping down in the striped chair. "Tell me," I plead. "Tell me everything."

Jil's palms are facing her shoulders and she's jerking her fingers about a million miles an hour. I wonder if this is what a heart attack looks like. Do kids have heart attacks? Is she fainting? Fanning? What?

"Take a deep breath," I say.

Jil inhales air from the tips of her toes all the way to the top of her head, then exhales for longer than the greatest singer on earth could possibly hold a note. Finished with that, she opens her mouth and starts a run-on sentence that would give Mr. Trimble, my English teacher, convulsions. Information spews out of her in one long speed report. It's as if Jil's suddenly the star witness at some trial of the century, but with a time limit.

"Okay," she says. "First, she wanted to know if it was really me, and I said yes, and she asked me again, and I said yes, only louder, and then she asked if my parents knew that I had called her, and I said no, and that made her kind of nervous. Major hesitation and her voice went real jittery. But then she got herself together again and asked me more stuff, and then she started talking about missing me, and loving me, and wondering about me, and I said me too, I'd been wondering about her—"

No, she didn't, I think. If she'd said "me too," I would've heard that. She just thinks she said "me too."

—"and she wants to meet me, but she says I *have* to tell my parents, and guess what?" She looks up at me, all excited—no more tears. "I can bring a friend. That's you, of course. And she lives about sixty miles away, in Greensboro, but we're going to meet here, in Durham, at Southpoint Mall, beside the big fountain. From there we'll pick one of those little outdoor tables, sit down, and get to know each other. Saturday, at three."

Suddenly, I'm excited too. My parents are my parents, so I have no idea what it feels like to know that there's someone else out there who, in some ways, is more your parent than your parents, but in most ways, isn't your parent at all. That has to be weird. And Jil's happy, so I'm happy. And she's going to tell her mom and dad, who always let her do anything she wants, probably even this.

"Jil," I say, my grin just as big as hers, "this is so awesome!"

Then I remember the part about bringing a friend.

Do I want to go with her? Yes. No. Maybe.

Mostly no. I picture a scene that's super emotional. Or awkward. What if we run out of things to say?

But I can't let her go alone. What if her mother is some kind of weirdo? Would Jil be safe? Will I be safe? I'll ask the Lewises what they think. They'll know.

"When are you going to tell your parents?" I ask.

"Never," says Jil.

We had a huge fight after that, and now I'm sitting in my room, the one where the plaids totally clash with the stripes, and wondering if I'm a good friend or a bad friend. I told Jil I wouldn't go to meet her mother unless she told her mom and dad about it. She said I was a wuss and a traitor, and how could I ruin the most important thing that has ever happened to her in her life?

I got mad and said, "You're crazy—you know that? You have the best parents in the whole world."

"They're okay," she'd said.

"Okay! Okay? Are you kidding? They're great! I would trade with you in a second."

"So, trade," she said.

"*Yeah, right.*" I laughed. "I'd like to see you survive one day in my junky, cluttered, shoddy, shabby house."

"It's not any of those things," Jil sputtered. "It's comfortable."

Was she kidding? "It's the most mega-messy house on earth!" I'd shouted.

"It feels lived in," she answered, so calmly that it annoyed the heck out of me.

"*Your* house is elegant," I said, irritated, but meaning every word.

"Stifling," said Jil.

"Neat," I argued.

"Sterile."

I gave up then. It wasn't until I got home that I realized we'd somehow stopped comparing our parents and had begun complaining about our houses instead.

So now, I want to march back over there and explain to her how warm and friendly and loving her parents are. And she'll say mine are warm and friendly and loving too. And I'll say, "Yeah, but yours are normal. They take trips, play tennis, and vacuum. They have friends and a piano and do regular stuff. My dad quotes poetry and reads moldy books. My mother mucks around in swamps, collects dustballs the size of cows, and watches the weather channel like it's *Sex and the City*."

But it's nine o'clock and I know my parents won't let me go back out. I don't want to call or e-mail. This needs to be face-to-face. It's that important.

So I stretch out on my bed and think about the birthday party that Jil's about-to-be-replaced parents gave her when she was ten. It was a Pixie Slumber Party, just for girls, with invitations delivered on rolled-up parchment paper printed with fancy, curly writing, tied up in satin ribbons the color of emeralds.

We all wore beautiful, slippery, soft nightgowns that

Mrs. Lewis had found on sale somewhere and let us keep. As soon as the sun went down, the Lewises put real flowers in our hair, gave us magic wands, fairy flutes, and maps of Pixieland, which turned out to be Jil's uncle's farm. Three snow-white ponies led us in a procession to the top of a hill, where we swirled and danced, caught fireflies, and ate fairy berries and melt-in-your-mouth chocolate cupcakes made to look like toadstools covered in frost.

It was magic.

For *my* tenth birthday, my parents suggested I invite friends over to cut dirty raw potatoes into weird shapes, ink them, and stamp them on T-shirts. "Tater T-shirts" they called them. It was something they'd learned from their tie-dying years.

I told them about Jil's moonlit pony party, and Mom said, "Amazing."

Dad said, "How extraordinarily whimsical. We could do something like that. Let's call it *A Midsummer Night's Dream*, and act out scenes from Shakespeare, and—"

"Potatoes will be fine," I'd said.

Now, I roll over and think about going to sleep, but it's still only nine o'clock. Should I start one of my new library books?

Yesterday, after English class, I'd asked Mr. Trimble if he knew any good books about faraway, exotic places.

Jil's parents have taken her to a million cool places: New York, Hawaii, Mexico, Switzerland. My parents

never go anywhere, not because they can't afford to—
they can—but because they'd just rather stay home. Dad
says books will take me anywhere I want to go.

Once, he gave me *Pride and Prejudice* by Jane Austen,
and it took me to England. I loved it, but I would never
tell him that.

So Mr. Trimble asked me if I'd ever read Mark Twain's
travel journals.

"Fiction," I told him. "I want fiction, preferably by
authors who haven't won awards and aren't famous."
What I'd meant by that was that I wanted a book a kid
would like, not one a teacher would pick.

Then he asked me if I'd read any Batchelder Award
books, and I answered, "Never heard of them," and he
said, "Try them. They're set in foreign countries. It's an
award for great books that have been translated into
English but were originally published in another language."

It still sounded suspiciously teacherly to me, but since
I was never going to get to Italy or Africa or China any
other way, I decided to give one a try.

I creep over to my bookshelf and stare at the three
books I'd picked. I'd chosen three, not because I thought
I'd actually read three books in the two weeks before
they'd be due back at the library, but because if I hated
the first one, I'd have a couple of spares to fall back on.

Carefully, I pull out *Samir and Yonatan*. I like to
arrange my books from tallest to shortest so they look

neat on the shelf. The flap says it's about an Israeli boy and a Palestinian boy who become friends in spite of their differences. What I do not need right now is a book about tough friendships. I slide it back into its slot.

The other two are *The Thief Lord*, which sounds exciting and takes place in Venice, and *The Shadows of Ghadames*, which sounds like it might be boring, until I read the front flap again and remember that it's about a girl who wants to travel with her father but she's stuck at home because girls in her country aren't allowed to go anywhere, not even out their front doors. The only way she even gets to see the city that she lives in is from her rooftop.

I pull it out from the shelf, then slide all the other books over to fill in the gap. Clearly, here is a girl with problems worse than mine. I decide to read it, hoping she'll get to travel after all, and I'll discover how she manages it. And because I want to know what an African city in Libya looks like from a rooftop.

By the time I read two chapters, I decide that I need to be stronger.

Tomorrow, when Jil calls and says, *Dez, you have to help me*, for the first time in my life, I'm going to say no.

Chapter Seven

I feel like such a fool.

Jil did call, just like I knew she would. And begged me to go with her to the mall to meet her mother. I said, "Not unless you tell your parents."

At the time, saying that had made me feel great, in spite of the fact that I could be losing Jil's friendship forever. *And* access to normal parents and a piano.

But I thought I might be saving her from a possible psycho. And keeping her from hurting her parents. I also figured she would never go alone.

Wrong. Wrong. Wrong.

She went. And guess what? Her mom's a perfectly nice person. No knife hidden in her purse. No crazy twitching or babbling. Just a small woman with blond hair like Jil's.

And when she got home, Jil told her parents everything.

And according to Jil, they weren't hurt at all.

I wonder if that's true.

Anyway, she was so excited that she even forgave me for being a jerk. She called later that night, just to tell me how great her new mom was. And that she was short, just like her. They even had the same blue eyes.

"Dez!" Jil had exclaimed. "She looks like me! And guess what? I've got a sister! A half sister. She's ten and her name is Penny and her nose turns up just like mine. We haven't met yet, but I saw her picture."

I figure the main reason she ended up telling her parents was because she wanted to spend the night with Mom-2 and meet the new sister, and no way could she invent a good enough plan to pull that off without her usual accomplice—me.

"What do you call her?" I asked.

"Mom."

"What do you call your old mom?"

"Mom."

"Doesn't that get confusing?"

"Not to me."

I hesitated, not sure I should bring up the next thing on my mind. "Was your dad there?" I asked anyway.

"He's gone. Split for Alaska or somewhere before I was even born." Jil said this as calmly as she might have mentioned that they happened to be out of bananas.

"Does Penny have a dad?" I asked in a way that I hoped sounded concerned, because I was concerned.

"He died."

"Oh."

What I really wanted to hear were details about how her parents had taken all this great news, because, no matter what Jil claimed, I imagined them pretty hurt.

"What'd your parents say?" I whispered. I hadn't meant to whisper, but somehow my words slipped out that way.

"They were supportive!" exclaimed Jil, excited again. "Super supportive, even," she added.

I pictured her cradling the phone between her shoulder and her ear so that she could extend her hands out, fingers spread in convincing celebration. Did I believe her? I wanted to, because the thought of the Lewises being sad or hurt made my throat ache.

"They want me to be happy, Dez! They understand that I need to know."

"That's great, Jil!" Maybe it *was* true. I was amazed. So amazed that I blurted, "But aren't they really mad at Mom-2?"

"Who? What? Dez! Don't call her that."

"Sorry," I apologized. "I didn't mean anything bad by that, honest. But, hey! I've got to call her *something*. How will you know who I'm talking about?"

"Oh," said Jil, then proudly added, "Jane."

"Jane?"

"That's her name. Jane Simmons. But 'Mrs. Simmons' sounds wrong somehow. Too proper. So call her Jane."

I hate it when you can't see a person's face, but Jil sounded as if she were relaxed and smiling again, so I took a chance and repeated my original question. "Okay. It's Jane. But, Jil, don't your parents want to strangle her?"

She laughed.

I relaxed and resumed breathing.

"No. Because I let them know how she'd refused to

meet me unless I told them. I confessed that I'd lied to get her to come to the mall."

"And they're okay?"

"Yeah."

"Really?"

"They're fine, Dez. Honest. They met and talked with Mom. They're going to let me visit her."

"They should win the Parents of the Year Award. You know that, don't you?"

"I guess."

"You *guess*!?" Now *I* was annoyed.

"Dez, don't start."

"Sorry. Can I go with you sometime?"

"I think for a while it should just be me. Okay?"

"Sure."

So I had stuck to what I thought was right for *nothing*. Everything turned out fine, and I missed meeting her mom. For *nothing*.

I can't wait to meet Jane. And Penny.

Jil can't stop talking about how cool they are. Jane lets her stay up late, put sugar on Cocoa Puffs, and she and Penny hang out at the mall all day.

Meanwhile, Mrs. Lewis is teaching me to play the piano. I can go there and practice, even when Jil's not home. So everybody's happy.

Except my parents. You should have heard them when I told them all this. We were all sitting at the kitchen table, eating spaghetti. Denver looked like he'd taken a bath in tomato sauce. Then he knocked over his milk, drenched his shirt, and started shrieking.

"'*Pour the sweet milk of concord into hell, uproar the universal peace,*'" Dad recited. Then he winked at me and said, "William Shakespeare," to let me know that he was the dead poet he'd just quoted.

"Don't say 'hell' in front of Denver," said Mom. "You know how he repeats things." Then to Denver she said, "Shhh, sweetie. Don't cry over spilled milk."

I sat up straight, stuck my chin out, and leveled Dad with a challenging stare. "'*I spilled my milk, and I spoiled my clothes, and I got a long icicle hung from my nose!*' Mother Goose." Then I winked back.

Dad and I have this thing where we have poetry duels. He quotes some old guy whose poetry doesn't even rhyme, and then I hit him with something better. At least I think it's better. Dad claims that my stuff is verse, not poetry, and it may be fun, but it's not serious. And that I should learn the difference.

I *have* learned the difference. Mine's better.

Anyway, while Mom washed Denver with a dish towel that looked older than one of Dad's poets, I told them about Jil.

"Dez," Mom said. "You need to be a good friend. Jil may be skating on thin ice."

"What's that supposed to mean?"

"It means her relationship with her mother may not turn out as well as you think."

"*'And oft, though wisdom wake, suspicion sleeps at wisdom's gate,'*" muttered Dad, shaking his head.

"Look. It's fine. Honest. The Lewises are being supportive. I know. I saw Mrs. Lewis yesterday. She gave me a piano lesson and she wasn't crying or anything. And Jane and Penny are cool."

"She gave you another piano lesson?" said Mom, tossing the sauce- and milk-stained towel in the same corner as the coffee-stained towel and the berry-stained towel. Right next to the harder-than-a-board slice of American cheese that had been sitting out since yesterday.

"Yeah—she says I can come over as much as I want. I'm learning 'Moonlight Sonata.' By Beethoven. He's an old dead guy, Dad. You'd love him."

"I know who Beethoven is," Dad said, raising one eyebrow at me.

"I don't want you imposing on Mrs. Lewis," said Mom.

"Okay," I answered brightly. "Can I have a piano, then? Please? I'll pay for my own lessons."

"With what?" they both asked at the same time.

"I don't know. I'll earn it. Somehow. I will."

"Don't bite off more than you can chew," said Mom.

"Neither a borrower nor a lender be," said Dad.

I wasn't sure how either one of those particularly fit what we were talking about, so I just answered, "Red fish, Blue fish," and went back to eating my spaghetti.

Parents know nothing.

Chapter Eight

I've given up "Moonlight Sonata" until further notice.

I still love to play the opening *tah-dah-dah*s, but it's way too hard a piece for a beginner like me. Mrs. Lewis makes me feel great about it, though.

"Dez," she says. "I love to see how hard you're working at this."

"Thanks."

She sits next to me on the bench, so close I can smell her perfume. She holds my sweaty hands in her manicured ones and says, "You have a pianist's hands—long and slender. It's exciting to see someone your age so interested."

She stares across the room at an oil painting of a cottage with a beautiful flower garden, but I don't think she sees it. I think she's wishing that Jil liked the piano as much as I do, and that Jil were here instead of at her other mom's. I also think I see tears floating in her eyes.

Has Mrs. Lewis been supportive? Maybe.

Is she sad? Definitely.

Then she snaps out of it and continues. "But, Dez, I don't think even Mozart began by playing a sonata."

"Oh. Okay," I answer. "What then?"

"How about scales and maybe one or two simple melodies?"

So, now I'm practicing scales to figure out how to make my fingers work, and Mrs. Lewis is teaching me "Jingle Bells" in time for Christmas.

The Lewises always have this incredible party two days before Christmas and invite the whole neighborhood. Their entire house is decorated with tapered white candles and deep green garlands of fresh pine branches that make everything smell the way Christmas is supposed to. The tree is gigantic, covered with amazing ornaments of every shape and color. My favorite is a tiny black glass piano that looks so fragile I think my breath could break it if I stood too close.

At the party, Mr. Lewis always opens his front door looking handsome and saying, "Welcome! Merry Christmas!" over and over, but sounding like he really means it, every single time. Then he asks each guest if he can take his or her coat, which makes me feel exceptional—and older. Not old enough for the adult eggnog though. That is completely off-limits because a fifth of whiskey has been dumped into it.

Two years ago, when we were only eleven, Jil and I sneaked a taste. We totally agreed the kids' drink was better, except for the fact that the adults' version floats in a huge crystal punch bowl. The kiddy eggnog gets served in a pretty pitcher that has tiny candy canes etched all over it. But pouring from it is nowhere near as elegant as picking up a sterling silver ladle and scooping creamy liquid out of a crystal bowl five times bigger than the biggest mixing bowl on earth.

And . . . Food. Is. Everywhere.

Beautiful, yummy, catered, and completely different every year. Plus, kids under ten get to take home gifts wrapped in shiny white paper with red satin bows. The last year that I got one, before I aged out, it was a box filled with Hershey's Kisses, each one wrapped in red foil. I know it's the same candy that comes in ordinary plastic bags from Eckerd's, but when you nestle a bunch of kisses in a box with crisp white tissue paper, they taste better.

Toward the end of every party, Mrs. Lewis, looking like a movie star, always plays the piano while everyone circles around her and sings Christmas carols.

On December 23, going to the Lewises is as good as it gets.

I don't mean to sound bratty and horrible, because I love Christmas at my house, too. But the differences are staggering. There's no pine smell here because our tree is fake and stays in the attic, decorated all year. When it comes out, it takes me all day to pick away dust balls and pieces of pink attic insulation that get on everything. I have to wear those thick yellow dishwashing gloves to protect my fingers from the tiny strands of insulation that act like invisible splinters of glass.

Our holiday food is the packaged-fruit-cake and pre-cooked-turkey-breast-with-canned-gravy variety, and most of our presents are wrapped in recycled gift bags. We've never had a party, except for the Tater T-shirts kind, and Dad has definitely never asked anyone under twenty if he could take her coat.

Jil says my decorations are better, though, and she's right. They aren't as beautiful as hers, even after I clean them up each year, but every one has its own story, like the baby-food jar lid with my picture pasted inside that I made in first grade. Or the dangling strand of cheap pink-and-purple beads that Mom and Dad bought from a street vendor the year they met. Denver has a purple-and-yellow turtle that he painted himself. I have a needlepoint St. Lucia—it's Swedish—that I made when my Sunday school created a Holidays Around the World tree.

If you ask me, Christmas is one of those times that's special no matter how you do it.

So, imagine my surprise when I call Jil, three days before her party, and she tells me that she won't be there.

"Huh?"

"I'm going to my mom's," she says, sounding all bubbly.

"Your mom's? Mom-2?"

"Don't call her that."

"Sorry. You're going to Jane's? For Christmas?" I exclaim.

"No, silly," she says. "I'll be back by Christmas Eve."

I decide she's kidding. "Yeah, right," I say.

"No, really. I am. Mom and Penny are going to have their whole Christmas early. Just for me. It's going to be awesome!"

"Wow."

It's not much, but honestly, it's all I can think of to say. Ever since Jil found her mom, I've been excited for her. Maybe even a little jealous. But *not going to her own Christmas party*? That takes this two-family deal to a whole new level.

"Kids from divorced families do this all the time," she explains in the same tone of voice that the TV might say, "Clothes cleaned with Tide are whiter and brighter, every single wash." It reminds me of her Christopher Columbus voice, the one that's always been reserved for convincing adults. This is the first time it's ever been used on me.

Which bugs me. But then Mom's *friend-in-need* warning goes off inside my head.

"Your mom's letting me play 'Jingle Bells'!" I chirp with outward enthusiasm. Inside, I'm not only still annoyed, but I'm also feeling pretty majorly sorry for myself because Jil won't be there to hear my official debut as an artist. Or to sneak a sip of gross-tasting adult egg-nog and make gagging noises with me.

"I know. I'm really sorry I won't be there," she says, not sounding like a commercial anymore, but sad, as if she truly is sorry. "But you can play it for me when I get back. Okay?"

"Definitely." I hope I sound convincing. "Have fun. I'll miss you."

"Me too. See ya!"

Three days later, December 23, I arrive at the Lewises with my parents. I'm super nervous because I want to sound good for them on the piano. I only know how to play the "Jingle Bell" melody—no chords—but it's important that I get it right so they'll know I'm serious about wanting a piano.

When I practice alone, I get so excited about the song that's magically coming out of my very own fingers that I swear I feel icy wind chilling my face. I hear laughing and singing and one-horse-open-sleigh runners gliding across soft snow. I even hear bells on bobtails ring, and I have not one single clue what a bobtail is. But I want my parents to hear it too.

They're still calling my piano playing *a passing phase*, but I know better.

Mr. Lewis flings the front door wide open and greets my family. "Welcome, Denver! Merry Christmas, Dez! Scott! Linda! So glad you could come." The aromas of warm candles, hot roast beef, and freshly baked bread fill the foyer while Mr. Lewis ushers us in from the cold as though we're royalty. He's wearing a Christmas tie with tiny reindeer on it, and a red handkerchief neatly tucked into the chest pocket of his sport coat. The coat fits him so perfectly, he looks as if he stepped straight out of a fashion magazine. Dad doesn't have on a jacket, but he is wearing a white dress shirt with a cool bow tie, and even though the shirt's a little wrinkled, he looks good . . . for Dad.

Mom is not in her gray sweats. She does own a dress. Maybe two. This one's shiny and the color of a dark ruby. I think it would look a lot better if she hemmed it four inches shorter, but she just hugs me and says, "Dez, I'm happy that you care. Really, I am." Then she adds, "The true meaning of Christmas has nothing to do with fashion."

I know that. I'm not stupid. But, still . . . I doubt that God meant for the whole human race to walk around wadded up in swaddling clothes, either. Despite her no-style statement, Mom's dangly earrings match her dress, and from the hemline up, she looks good. Better than good, she looks neat. Who knew she owned earrings?

I'm feeling almost proud of them, which is way better than the usual embarrassment, but I wonder—if they've noticed how to dress for the Lewises, why don't they notice how good a living room looks without mildewed stacks of magazines in the corners? Or Legos and Mr.

Potato Head parts covering every inch of the carpet? Or how clean a kitchen counter is when there's no faded shoe box full of old batteries and rusty nails sitting on it? Or how fantastic a real Christmas tree smells?

"May I take your coat?" asks Mr. Lewis, bowing slightly from the waist.

I feel like a princess.

Except that the coat in question is my bulky quilted nylon jacket with a rip in one sleeve—torn while assisting in the attempted-but-unsuccessful theft of a street sign.

That's okay, though. Underneath, I'm wearing a dynamite outfit. Slinky black pants that flare at the bottom, tiny hot pink heels, and a silvery scoop-neck top. For the first time ever, I feel confident that tall looks good.

Mr. Lewis reminds Denver and me that all the kids are in the downstairs rec room. "You know the way," he says cheerfully, then turns to talk to my parents.

Denver sprints for the basement, and I follow. There's a lady there who snags Denver immediately and herds him off to a corner where all the under-fives are busy coloring candy-cane pictures. Silently, I wish her luck.

Glancing around, I'm not surprised to find food, games, and even a miniature version of the upstairs Christmas tree. I hang out, nibbling chips with dip and tender, juicy chicken chunks skewered on little sticks of bamboo. I play one game of Ping-Pong, sip homemade eggnog from a plastic Santa cup, and miss Jil.

Feeling the jitters of my "Jingle Bells" performance

beginning to creep over me, I wander back upstairs to stare at the piano—for calming purposes. And to make sure all the keys are right where I left them.

"Dez!" exclaims Mrs. Lewis. "You look amazing!"

"Thanks," I say, admiring the simple black silk dress that she's accented with a string of white pearls. A pair of fantastic-looking high heels tells me that her feet are covering a New York designer label with a name I can't pronounce. "You look pretty amazing too."

She gives me a quick hug, then takes me by the hand. "Follow me."

Expertly, she guides me through four groups of people and into the dining room. Grown-ups are standing around talking about what they found on sale at the last minute, who's coming to their Christmas Day dinners, and why they really shouldn't eat any more little tarts filled with crabmeat, while they scarf down two more anyway.

Mrs. Lewis takes the Santa cup out of my hand and reaches for one of the crystal cups beside the adult eggnog bowl.

She's going to give me alcohol? No way!

I'm speechless.

Then she takes my Santa cup and pours its kiddy contents into the beautiful cut-crystal cup. "Performing artists should not have to drink out of plastic," she says.

The cup is heavy in my hand. It feels extravagant and solid. I don't mind that she didn't put whiskey in it. To tell you the truth, I'm relieved. That would mean that she was a crummy parent, and then what would I say to convince Jil?

"These cups were my great-grandmother's," she says. "She brought them with her all the way from Italy, wrapped in a patchwork quilt."

"Thanks, Mrs. Lewis." I take a sip of my eggnog. "It tastes better!"

I have just graduated from feeling like a princess to queen status. I'm also thankful to know that Jil does have Christmas things with stories.

I wander into the living room and eye the piano. It's even shinier than normal. I bet I could pluck my eyebrows in the reflection—if I plucked my eyebrows. The whole room is elegant. White-blooming poinsettia plants and twinkling lights everywhere.

Being careful not to make eye contact, I slip through two groups of people so I can work my way into the corner with the Christmas tree and not have to answer a dozen neighbors, who will all ask, "How's school?" I scan all the awesome ornaments, looking for my favorite. The glass piano. It's so tiny, maybe it's tucked behind—

"Attention!" Mr. Lewis shouts into the crowd. "May I have everyone's attention, please?" He raps a spoon against his crystal eggnog cup to quiet the roomful of party people.

My mind screams, *Don't! You'll break the great-grandmother's cup!*

Eventually, the room quiets, and Mr. Lewis clears his

throat. "Thank you all for coming. It just wouldn't be Christmas without each and every one of you." Then he bows his head and begins a prayer: "Bless this house on this very special night. May we all keep this spirit in our hearts. . . ."

I bow my head with the rest of the people in the room, but I don't hear the whole prayer. My brain gets stuck on the *it wouldn't be Christmas without each and every one of you* part.

If Jil were here, I would hit her.

Stupid—if Jil were here, I wouldn't need to hit her.

"Amen."

"And now," says Mrs. Lewis, clapping her hands together. "Who wants to sing?"

Everyone makes a move to circle the piano.

"But first"—she beams across the room at me—"we have a promising new pianist in our midst, who, after only two weeks of lessons, is going to play 'Jingle Bells.'"

My gut seizes up like a fist.

"Ladies and gentlemen"—she gracefully unfolds her arms in my direction—"I give you Destiny Carter!"

Chapter Nine

I sit at the piano and stare at my hands.

Don't look up, I warn myself. Don't look at the ocean of expectant faces. Just play. Plunk out the notes. You can do it.

So I plunk some notes. *Dashing through the snow: plink-plink, plink-plink-plink.* I sound like a toy piano. Suddenly, I wish I knew chords.

But then I get the single notes to flow better. And, miraculously, I am on a one-horse open sleigh, o'er the fields I go, laughing all the way.

The next thing I know, there's applause, and Denver is shouting, "That's my sister," and some man is yelling, "Once more time from the top!"

So I start over and everyone sings along, which is way harder because of the timing, but somehow I do it, only hitting one wrong note. Amazingly, no one seems to notice.

Mrs. Lewis slides in next to me and adds chords to my notes. Wow. Now I sound really good, but the timing is impossible—staying in sync with her chords *and* with fifty booming voices! I want out of here! Now!

Mrs. Lewis, mind reader, leans over and whispers, "Dez. You were wonderful. Ready to take a break?"

Gratefully, I slip off the piano bench and leave it to Mrs. Lewis, who somehow segues from "Jingle Bells" straight into "Hark the Herald Angels Sing." The entire room belts out the words with mega-decibels and joy.

You wouldn't believe how many people in our neighborhood actually know the second verse to "Away in a Manger." And all *four* verses of "Silent Night." Half of them pat me on the back and whisper things like, "Good job, Dez," "You're a natural," or "Imagine—you learned that in only two weeks!"

Apparently, the Carter family is multiskilled—Dad is the only one in the room who can sing "O Come, All Ye Faithful" in Latin. Every single verse. Right now I feel as if that's a pretty cool talent, but I'll need to be ready to take some serious junk about it when school starts again in January.

I sing.

Between "Away in a Manger" and "The First Noel," I sip more eggnog from my beautiful crystal cup. I feel like I just won *American Idol*.

I'm still floating on air after Mr. Lewis has retrieved my coat, and both he and Mrs. Lewis have waved good-bye to me and my family with choruses of "Merry Christmas! So happy you came! Thank you for playing, Dez! Great Latin solo, Scott! Brilliant purple candy-cane picture, Denver!"

At the last minute, Mrs. Lewis sneaks a small box wrapped in white paper and tied with red satin ribbon into my hands.

"But I'm too old," I protest.

"You're just old enough," she whispers, gives me a nudge toward the door, then turns to say good-bye to the Paulo family.

At home, we all gather in the den. Dad unsnaps his bow tie and slides it off through his shirt collar. I pick a handful of Denver's fairy-tale puzzle pieces off the sofa and put them in their correct slots. Then I flop down. "The Lewises are so much fun," I say.

"Especially their eggnog," says Dad, shooting me a meaningful look that has no meaning to me at all.

"What? You don't drink alcohol," I say, puzzled.

"And from this day forward, neither do you, young lady."

"Huh?" When Dad calls me *young lady*, it's bad.

"Dez," says Mom. "Come on. We saw you drinking from the nice cups. I certainly didn't want to make a scene there, but—"

"Wait! No! No way. That was the kiddy stuff. Honest."

After I explain what Mrs. Lewis had done, they both react with such relief you'd think they'd just learned that I wasn't an ax murderer after all.

"Thank God," says Mom. Her words shoot out in one giant super-sigh of relief.

Dad says, "I was afraid you'd be too drunk to play the piano."

"*You thought I was drunk?*" I shriek.

"Dez drunk," says Denver. "Drunk. Drunk. Drunk." His hands beat the coffee table like a drum in time to his chant. Then he looks up and says, "What's drunk?"

"Young man," grumbles Dad, "it's time for you to go to bed."

Yay. Denver is *young man* now, which takes the heat off me being *young lady*. Then it hits me. They actually thought I was guzzling alcohol at a neighborhood Christmas party! Can you believe that? Okay. I admit, I did taste the spiked eggnog a couple of years ago, but just a taste. And it was terrible. *And*, I *sneaked* it. I'm not stupid!

"I'm not going," Denver announces, standing up and jamming his hands on his hips.

"Oh, but thou art," says Dad. "It's way past your bedtime."

"Not 'til Dez plays 'Jingle Bells' again," Denver pleads. "Pleeeeeze."

I'd be a fool to say what I'm thinking now, which is, "I'd love to play 'Jingle Bells' again, but we don't have a piano." Followed by, "Bless you, Denver."

"She was good wasn't she?" says Dad, clearing a space so he can sit down on his brown leather recliner.

"You were *very* good," Mom says to me as she stoops down to carry Denver bodily from the room.

"Does that mean we can buy a piano?"

"No," she says on her way out of the room. I can barely hear her over Denver's sobbing, but I do hear.

No, even when a child is screaming over it, doesn't sound anything like yes.

"Why not?" I complain.

"A piano costs a lot of money," says Dad.

I guess I should be grateful that he didn't answer me in Greek.

"How much money?"

"A lot."

"More than your fifty million boxes of smelly old books?"

Dad leans back in his chair and raises his eyebrows. Which is my signal to shut up, but I don't.

"We could rent a piano. Or buy a used one. I'll get a job. I'll—"

"Dez," says Dad. "Your mother and I aren't convinced that this new passion of yours will last. Remember the vio—"

"But it will, Dad, I know it will. What do I have to do to convince you?"

Dad pops his recliner into lie-back position and reaches for his *Journal of Dead Poets*, or whatever boring magazine he's got handy.

"You'll have to stick with it. *''Tis known by the name of perseverance in a good cause—and of obstinacy in a bad one.'*"

Good grief.

When Mom finally rejoins us, wearing her gray sweats, she shoves a bunch of newspapers onto the floor and lies down on the sofa. As she props her sock feet up onto a pillow, she switches to the Weather Channel.

"About the piano," I say.

"Not now, honey. Besides, you need to show some interest for a lot longer than two weeks. You know, keep your nose to the grindstone, stick to your guns—"

I can tell she's searching for another cliché, but *Storm Stories* flickers onto the TV screen, and I know I've lost her for the night.

In my room, I open my closet door and hang up my coat. Then I sit down at my desk, open the top drawer, and arrange all the pens and pencils in it according to color. That looks dumb, so I move them around according to size. Better.

Tonight, I had practically a standing-ovation piano debut, and my parents want more proof. They want me to show interest longer.

How much longer? Ten years, like the Trojan War? More, like the amount of time dinosaurs roamed the earth?

What I could use right now is a friend. Or chocolate. I wonder what Jil is doing at this very minute. I picture her laughing. Hugging. Getting presents from family number two. Then I remember Mrs. Lewis's gift, and reach for this year's box of Hershey's Kisses. Or maybe she gave M&M's this time. Or Sour Patch Kids. Except it feels too light for any of those things. Whatever, I know it'll taste good. Sugary. Comforting.

I untie the red ribbon. Then I roll it into small, smooth loops, which I secure with a paper clip, and place it neatly into my desk drawer. Carefully, I slide my finger under the tape to remove the wrapping paper without tearing it.

I open the box, and reaching into the tissue paper, I immediately feel something soft. It's cotton—a big cushiony layer of cotton like the stuff clerks put in jewelry boxes. Confused, I lift it up and discover the Lewises' tiny black glass piano. The hand-blown ornament they got on their trip to Switzerland. My favorite.

I hold it in my hands, almost afraid to breathe. I can't believe it's mine. But I know in a second that this ornament will never hang on our tree. Not on the tree that gets banged around and stuffed into the attic to get covered in dust every year.

I touch each delicate piano leg, marveling at the detail and the fragileness. I bet it was made by a master Swiss craftsman.

Maybe I'll decorate my own tree. A real one. Miniature, like the one in the Lewises' basement. For my room only.

An ache rises up in the back of my throat and I feel a tear spill over and slip slowly down my cheek.

But I'm *happy*. Aren't I? So . . . why am I crying?

Holding the piano as if it were a snowflake, I lie down on my bed, faceup, and wish with all my heart that the Lewises were my parents.

Chapter Ten

January 4—my first day back at school, and so far, nobody's remembered to make fun of my father's Latin solo.

Yay.

I remember too vividly some of the nicknames they've tagged my parents with in the past. Papa Poet. Swamp Mama.

I look everywhere for Jil, whom I barely saw over the entire Christmas vacation.

"Graham!" I shout, spotting him standing in front of his locker. "Hey!"

Graham is one of the few eighth-grade boys who is actually taller than I am. Too bad he's not my type. Way too messy. But he's really cute—if you don't mind all the holes in his clothes.

I do mind. Which is a good thing, because, after all, he is Jil's boyfriend, not mine.

"Hey, Dez," he says, trying to slam his locker door shut with his shoulder but without success because way too many papers are hanging out. "What's up?"

I wonder if I should offer to clean out his locker sometime.

Of course not, Dez, I answer my own question. Years ago, I learned to keep the fact that I am a neat-oholic to myself. Messy is cool if you're a kid. Messy is not cool if you're a parent. I'm caught in a reverse generation warp. Who makes up these stupid rules, anyway?

"Have you seen Jil?" I ask.

"Nope."

"How'd you like the wallet?"

"What wallet?"

"The wallet Jil gave you for—" Uh-oh. I stop myself midsentence.

"A wallet, huh?" he says with a goofy grin on his face. "So that's what I would've gotten for Christmas if she hadn't dumped me?"

"Graham," I say. "I'm so sorry. I didn't know."

When I find Jil, I will kill her. After all, I talked to her Christmas Day. Before she and her parents left for their ski trip. Somewhere between all the stories of how great her Christmas was, and how great her new family is, and how great her new skis are, she could've mentioned that Graham was history, couldn't she?

"Nah, it's okay," says Graham. "Really. This is good to know. I thought she broke up with me because she didn't want to spring the extra bucks for a present. So"—he rolls his shoulders around like he needs to loosen up for the Olympics—"she'd already bought me something." He nods and repeats, "This is good to know."

He goes back to pushing his locker door. For a minute, I consider telling him how hard she tried to steal a street sign for him, but decide against it.

"Leather?" he asks.

"What?"

"The wallet. Was it leather? I mean, was it a good brand, like Coach, or something cheap?"

No wonder she broke up with him.

Graham's eyes get big. "No, wait." Like a cop trying to stop traffic, he pushes his open hand toward me. "That sounded wrong."

No kidding.

"I don't care how much it cost." He kicks his locker. "I just can't figure out why she dumped me. So, I just thought, if she got me an expensive present, then she really did like me. But if she got me a crummy present, then maybe she never cared in the first place, or—"

"She cared," I blurt. "She cared so much she could've gone to jail for you."

"What?" Graham looks at me the way I stare at Dad when he speaks Aramaic.

I fill him in on the freezing rain, the snow, me ripping my coat, and the street sign that we didn't steal. He nods and grins, so I guess my story makes getting dumped less painful. What I don't tell him is that Jil never keeps any boyfriend for very long. But he should already know that.

I leave Graham still trying to slam his locker shut, and

head for the library to return my books. Hoping Jil will be there.

I'm returning the book about the girl on the rooftops, which I finished. It didn't provide one single good plan for getting parents to take you on trips, but I did get a free make-believe trip to Libya out of it. Caravans, palm groves, and scorpions are way different from traffic, Southpoint Mall, and mosquitoes.

Maybe I'll renew the other two books—the ones I didn't get around to reading. I have a feeling that I'm about to have a lot of extra time to kill. After all, my best friend is never home anymore, and last night, Mom and Dad decided I can't impose on Mrs. Lewis and her piano more than twice a week.

Which is so unfair.

I told them that she loves for me to come over. They said she's being polite.

I said she misses Jil. They said that is not something I can fix.

I said they don't know anything. They said go to your room.

I have other friends, of course. There's a bunch of people I hang out with at school, or meet at home basketball games or the movies. But Jil is the only one who gets to see inside the cave that is my house. She may think a messy house that reeks of cigarette butts and dead socks is comfortable, but the rest of my friends would think it stinks.

"Dez!" shouts Jil. "Wait up!"

"Jil!" For a split second, I'm excited, but now that I know she's alive and breathing, I'm instantly mad.

"Why didn't you tell me about Graham?" I scream.

Jil hurries over. "What? Oh. Sorry," she says. "You never liked him anyway. Remember?"

"But you could've at least—"

"Guess what?" she cuts me off. "Dad is letting Mom and Penny and me have all four of his tickets to the Duke–Carolina game!"

"What!" I shout. No way. The Duke–Carolina game is the biggest rivalry in college basketball. *Nobody* can get tickets to that game. Except the Lewises, who buy season tickets because they both went to the University of North Carolina. And because they donate big bucks to the Rams Club.

"I know it's still a month away, but—"

Who cares? I'm thinking—all four tickets! Jil, Mom-2, Penny. That's three. Jil's going to ask me to go with them. She's got to—Graham is toast. And finally! I'll get to meet her new family.

"Mom and Dad have to be out of town," she continues. "They're dying! Totally dying. They've never missed that game, but Dad's got this business thing in St. Louis and they *have* to go to it, so guess what?"

"You have all four tickets!" I shout. I've been to lots of Carolina games with the Lewises. NC State, Virginia, Maryland. But never the Duke game. We grab each other by the arms and jump up and down.

"And Mom says Penny can bring a friend!" Jil exclaims. "I can't wait."

I let go of her arms as though they've burned me.

"Dez," says Jil. "What's wrong?"

"*Penny's* bringing a friend?"

"Well, yeah. I wanted to ask you, but Mom reminded me that you've been to a million games, but Penny's never—"

"Mom/Jane said that, or Mom/Mom?" I ask her guardedly.

"Mom/Jane," she says. "Is that okay? I mean . . ." Jil stares at me, then slumps. "Oh, Dez, I'm sorry. I just thought you'd been to lots of Duke–Carolina games, and—"

"It's okay," I say, forcing a smile.

"You have, haven't you?" She looks dazed.

"Yeah," I lie. "Once."

"Really? Just once? Well"—she puts her hands back on my scorched arms—"you can definitely count on next year!"

"*ZZZZZZZZZZ!*" The buzzer rips the air to let us know we're about to be late for our next class.

As Jil hurries away, I shout at her back, "Come over after school. I want to hear about—"

But she's already gone.

At least she freaked out when she realized what she'd done. After all, I am her best friend.

Besides, Dad teaches at Duke. Maybe he'd hate it if I went and cheered my head off for Carolina. People at Duke hate people at Carolina. It's tradition.

Who am I kidding? I've been a Carolina fan ever since the Lewises took Jil and me to our first game when we were seven. We wore Carolina blue T-shirts, Carolina blue socks, and even tied Carolina blue ribbons in our hair. We stuck fake tattoos of little blue feet on our faces. Then we bought pom-poms and screamed, *"Go, Tar Heels!"* until we hyperventilated.

Dad could have cared less. Just because he's a professor at Duke doesn't mean he's a sports fan. The only giant rivalry he even knows about is the one between God and Satan in *Paradise Lost*, a three-hundred-page poem that, for no good reason, repeats everything the Bible already said in Genesis.

Besides. It's only a stupid game.

I wouldn't go if she begged me.

Four weeks later, I still wouldn't go if she begged me. And I still haven't had a chance to talk to her. Oh, sure, we IM and talk on the phone and at school, but I mean really talk. About important stuff. Like her new family—and her old family.

I go to the Lewises' twice a week to practice piano. On Saturdays, when Jil's usually with Mom-2, and again on Tuesdays, when Jil has volleyball practice, because that's the best time for Mrs. Lewis.

It's still unfair though. Just when my fingers get all limbered up and stretched out and used to finding the right keys, I have to go home and not come back for half a week. Mrs. Lewis is teaching me everything—even posture. Body centered. Elbows out just a little. Wrists flat.

Mom and Dad said we should pay her, but at least I talked them out of that bad idea. Mrs. Lewis would be so insulted if I gave her money. Don't they know that?

So I take her something each week, like a loaf of fresh bread from the bakery, or a few flowers from the grocery store. All of which dents my allowance, but it's worth it, because Mom and Dad will have to notice that I'm serious.

Won't they?

Mostly they notice the stupid stuff, though. Not the important things.

Like tonight, I'm cleaning up the dinner dishes while Mom gives Denver an emergency bath. He tried to juggle eggs. Dad hands me a dirty plate and asks me about my homework.

"A few math problems, and a poem," I say, squirting liquid soap into the sink, which is slowly filling up with water.

Dad freezes in the middle of passing me a gunky casserole dish with baked-on chars of lasagna stuck to the sides. "What kind of poem?" he asks.

I am so stupid! I have just informed my father, the poetry professor, that my homework involves a poem. I plunge my hands into the sink full of soapy water and know that I deserve whatever I get.

"Nothing much," I mutter in the general direction of my navel.

"What's your assignment?" he persists. "Read a poem? Write a poem?"

"Write a poem," I whisper.

"Wunderbar!" he exclaims. "They *are* teaching you something! What kind of poem?"

"A sonnet." I wish I could disappear down the garbage disposal.

"Ah," he approves. "I have a book of Shakespearean sonnets. We can read them together after we finish the dishes. You can hear the meter, feel the rhythm—"

"Thanks, Dad, but Mrs. Macon gave us a bunch of guidelines, and—"

"I thought Mr. Trimble was your English teacher."

"He is," I answer. "This poem is for History."

"You're writing a poem for History?" Dad puckers his mouth, making his beard twitch like a nervous red mouse.

"On Warren G. Harding," I explain.

"Warren G. Harding, the president?"

"Yeah."

"And that would be . . . because . . ." He waits for me to fill in the blank.

"Because everybody in the class got assigned a different president," I say.

He drops the plate he's holding onto the counter. "No!" he cries out, clearly in pain. "You don't write a sonnet about something assigned! You write a sonnet about something you feel in your soul."

"Dad," I say in my most convincing voice, "I *love* Warren G. Harding."

Dad glares at me and stomps over to the drawer where we keep the phone book. "I'm calling your teacher," he says, picking up the phone with one hand. With the other hand, he jerks open the drawer so hard, the whole thing flies out and lands on the floor.

Blam!

Dried-up Magic Markers, green twist ties, dry-rotted rubber bands, and old refrigerator magnets spill onto the floor.

Fiercely, he spits out a strange-but-powerful word that's probably a curse in Greek.

"Please, Dad, no. Don't call. You'll embarrass me. Just let me write the stupid sonnet. It's not important—"

Dad staggers as if he's taken an arrow through his heart.

"No. Wait," I add quickly. "*Sonnets* are important— just not this one. This one is for a History grade. Mrs. Macon thought it would be a fun way to learn facts. Something different. You know. Bring history to life." I'm talking faster than Denver can find dirt.

"*Facts.*" He exhales it slowly and sadly, the way some- one might say their grandmother died. He's staring at the telephone when it rings in his hand.

If Mom were here, she would say, *Saved by the bell.*

"It's for you." Dad hands me the phone and leaves the room, stooped like an old man.

I dry my hands and pick up the phone.

"Dez!" cries Jil. "Guess what!"

Before I have time to think, much less guess, she says, "Penny's friend has the flu so bad she's throwing up buckets. Can you come to the Duke–Carolina game tomorrow night?"

Chapter Eleven

I am sitting in row M, seat 8, under a sea of blue banners that represent all the championships the University of North Carolina has won. Twenty-three thousand screaming fans are blasting out more decibels than a million jets taking off. Dick Vitale is interviewing Coach Roy Williams, live on ESPN, right in front of me, and shouting, *"It's awesome, baby!"*

Sometimes people lie to themselves. Each and every one of those times that I swore I would never come to this game even if Jil had begged me, I was flat-out lying.

Did I know I was lying?

Probably. Deep down.

Mom-2 and Penny picked Jil and me up at my house, right on time. Since Jil's parents are out of town, she's going to spend the night with me after the game.

"You're going to love Mom and Penny!" Jil exclaimed just as her new family blew the horn to let us know they were in the driveway. Jil's saying that is no big deal, except that in the last hour she'd said "You're going to love Mom and Penny" fourteen times. I counted. But each time, she jerked on her earlobe.

Who was she trying to convince?

But as soon as I set eyes on Mom-2 and Penny, I could finally understand some of Jil's excitement. They all three looked alike. It was amazing. Not just the blue eyes and turned-up noses that Jil had already told me about. No. It wasn't any one feature so much as it was that they just *looked* alike. The whole petite, *cute-as-a-button* package.

It took about forty minutes to drive the fifteen miles to Chapel Hill because the game traffic was awful. For the first ten minutes, Jil and Mrs. Simmons both tugged at their earlobes. I guess nervous habits are inherited. But then we all settled in and talked and laughed. Mrs. Simmons and Penny talked the most. And Jil was right. They *are* nice.

Mrs. Simmons said she was glad to meet me, and then, yay! did *not* spend the next hour asking me all the dumb questions that grown-ups usually ask some poor kid they've just met. Like, How's school? What grade are you in? What's your favorite subject?

Instead, she told me all about Penny. How she likes school and gets good grades and loves math.

Then Penny told us all about her school and her dog named Patches and how she wants a horse for her birthday.

"I want a piano," I volunteered.

"That's nice," said Mom-2.

"Yeah," said Jil. "You should hear her. She can already play better than—"

"Penny's a wonderful rider," said Mom-2, "but I'm afraid a horse is out of the question. I mean, where would we put a horse?" She laughed this funny little laugh that sounded like a tiny machine gun, but cute.

Jil and I filled them both in on every detail we knew about Carolina basketball. We told them about our first game, and how we'd worn tar-heel tattoos—tiny blue feet with black circles on the heels—on our faces.

"Can I get one?" asked Penny.

"We'll all buy one," said Jane.

I was beginning to think of Mom-2 as *Jane*. She was more of a name than a number now that she had a face. Especially since it was Jil's face.

When we finally got inside the Smith Center, Jane and Penny ooohed and aaahed over the size of the huge domed building. Then we all got fake tattoos. Jane bought Penny two, one for each cheek, plus pom-poms. Jil and I each got one, and then we all went into the ladies' room to put them on. All four of us were laughing like little kids, and were so hyped about the game that I thought we might explode.

You could feel it in the air. Excitement. Everywhere. I mean really *feel* it. Like a vibration or a pulse. As if everyone in the building had tiny sparklers all over them, spewing electric energy in every direction.

So now we're in our seats. Taking everything in. All of it is blue.

We're passing a bucket of popcorn back and forth, and I'm picking up all the spilled pieces and putting them in a napkin to throw away later, when Jil yells, "Cut that out!"

"Cut *what* out?"

"Cleaning!" she shouts.

"Okay," I say. "I'll try." And I do try, but sometimes stuff like that happens without my knowing it.

Penny loves the ram, who is actually a student dressed in a soft blue costume with curly horns. He high-fived her on the way down the aisle. I guess it's hard to dress up as a heel with tar on it, so the UNC mascot is a ram.

She's loving the cheerleaders, too. They've already done so many backflips we've lost count. Right now, one of them is actually standing on the hand of a guy cheerleader, who, amazingly, is holding her straight over his head with one hand.

Suddenly the guy in the big ram costume saunters onto the court holding a huge toy gun that shoots free T-shirts into the crowd.

"Penny! Look!" Jane laughs her cute little machine-gun laugh and points at him.

Jil and I know better than to get excited. We've spent the last six years complaining about the fact that he never even aimed one in our direction.

Maybe Jane and Penny have brought us luck, because

all of a sudden the ram points the barrel straight up into the crowd where we're sitting.

Pop!

I see it, heading straight toward me. A T-shirt, rolled up like a magazine, shot out of a giant popgun. Just when I think it's going to sail over my head and land ten rows higher, it loses momentum and arcs practically into my outstretched arms. I grab for it at the same time Jil does. We both clutch opposite ends of the prize and fall back into our seats.

"We got it!" shouts Jil.

Everyone around us is smiling and saying, "Way to go, girls!"

I let go of my end and say, "Here, Jil. You take it." I'd kill to keep it, but after all, they're her tickets.

"No way," answers Jil. "We both caught it. Fair and square. We both keep it."

"Can I hold it?" says Penny.

"Sure." Jil hands her the shirt.

"How can we both keep it?" I ask. "Rip it in half?"

"No, silly," says Jil, shoving me playfully. "We'll take turns. You keep it for a week. I keep it for a week."

"Cool," I say. "Like when someone wins a trophy but they have to give it back at the end of the season so the next winner can have it."

"Exactly."

"Or like in that book, *The Sisterhood of the Traveling Pants*, when all those girls share the same pair of jeans."

Jil high-fives me and says, "Even better."

So we giggle and call ourselves the Sisterhood of the Traveling Shirt.

Then I notice that Penny has put on our blue-and-white shirt. Across the front, it says UNC TAR HEELS, NATIONAL CHAMPIONS. She's grinning like crazy, waving her pom-poms, and screaming, "Go, Carolina!"

Jane's laughing and clapping.

I nudge Jil and jerk my head toward Penny.

Jil stares for a minute, obviously wondering what it means that Penny is wearing our shirt.

"Uh, Penny," says Jil. "It's okay if you want to wear it. But . . . uh . . . it's our shirt, you know. Mine and Dez's."

"What?" shouts Penny.

The game has restarted and the crowd is so loud Jil's words get sucked up like dust in a tornado.

"*It's my shirt!*" shouts Jil.

"*I know! I know!*" Penny shouts back.

Satisfied, Jil and I go back to screaming, "Go, Heels!"

The game is incredible. All of it. With only five minutes left, the lead has switched twenty times. It's been tied twelve times. There have been at least eight awesome slam dunks, ten astounding where-did-he-come-from blocked shots, and so many bad calls from the short ref with slick hair that I've lost count.

Foul on number 34, signals the other referee, holding up three fingers on one hand, four on the other.

"What!" screams Jil. "He never touched him!"

"Booooo!" I circle my fingers around my mouth and roar my disgust.

"Get new glasses!" shouts Jane.

"Get a new job!" shouts the man behind me.

"Go to—"

The crowd noise swallows the rest of it, but I know what he said.

I turn to see if Penny knows what he said. Penny is *asleep*! Curled up in Jil's and my shirt, sleeping like a baby, with people screaming their heads off all around her.

Then I remember. It *is* late. And a school night. And she is only ten. But still . . . this is the Duke–Carolina game! And the score is tied!

Jane leans across Penny and shouts something into Jil's ear. Jil's face drains completely of color. She stares at Jane as if she's lost her mind. Frantically, Jil shakes her head. Then she points at Penny and says something I can't hear. Jane answers something back.

Jil returns to watching the game, cheering loudly with the crowd.

"What?" I shout at her, grabbing her arm and shaking it. "What'd she say?"

Jil faces me. Clearly embarrassed. "Jane wants to go home. It's past Penny's bedtime."

"What!" I scream. "But . . . but . . ." I search for words that will express my complete and utter amazement. Finally, I settle on, "What difference does it make? Penny's already asleep!"

"Exactly," shouts Jil. "I pointed that out."

So, apparently, we get to stay to the end of the game. I go back to stomping my feet and shouting support to the players, to the rafters, to anyone, to everyone.

With only two seconds left on the game clock, Carolina is up by three points. Duke has the ball, and their point guard is flying downcourt as fast as his feet will carry him. The crowd noise is deafening. Pandemonium is the only way to describe it.

Just over the midcourt line, the Duke player pulls up and fires a desperation three-pointer.

Twenty-three thousand people all hold the same breath.

The ball soars through the air forever, then arcs, drops, and swishes through the net. Clean. Like a dagger in my heart.

We're going to overtime.

The crowd sound switches from thunder to nothing. No sound at all. Not even a gasp.

Penny wakes up.

Jane says, "Sorry, girls. But we'll have to go now."

Chapter Twelve

"**C**an you believe it?" whispers Jil.

We're both lying in the dark, in my bedroom. Jil under the covers of one twin bed. Me in the other. Supposedly falling asleep.

"No," I grumble. "I can't."

As a matter of fact, I will *never* believe it. But I don't want Jil to feel any worse than she already does, so I try to find a bright side. "We could make it into the *Guinness Book of World Records*, you know."

"Huh? For what?"

"For being the only four people in the history of the universe who ever left a Duke–Carolina game at the beginning of overtime."

"What? Oh." Jil makes a nervous little rapid-fire noise that sounds chillingly like Mom-2's laugh—the laugh I thought was cute, but now I'm not so sure.

"No," says Jil, "what I meant was, can you believe we won the game?"

"Won it? I can't believe we missed it!" I hiss across the dark space between our beds.

"Oh, come on," says Jil. "You got to hear it on the radio."

Is she for real? The *radio*? I heard the most exciting finish in the history of college basketball on a radio? If I'd been home, at least I could have seen it on TV.

"Look. They had to drive all the way back to Greensboro," Jil says defensively. "That put them home a whole hour later than us, ya know. And it was late. And Penny's only ten."

The silence in the room is almost as deafening as the one that followed the three-point shot that sent the game into overtime. It's probably just as loud as the silence immediately before the second overtime. Maybe even before the third one.

But how would I know? I wasn't there.

Three overtimes! And I had to listen to all of them on a radio that was turned down so low—so as not to wake up the child who was still wearing my T-shirt—that I could barely hear it.

And then, when we got to my house, Jane says, "I hate to wake her up. Can you wait until next week to get your shirt?"

And Jil gulps and answers, "Okay."

I remember the gulp. I heard it. So, Jil does feel rotten about this whole thing. She has to. She just doesn't want to admit it.

Okay, I think. I can relate to that. Embarrassing family members. I can relate to that totally.

"I'm sorry," I apologize into the dark of the room. "It is a school night. And they probably have no clue how big that game is."

Jil's sheets rustle. I hear a tiny whimper. The sheets rustle again.

"Jil?"

"Yeah."

"Are you crying?"

"No." Her voice cracks.

"Yes, you are."

"Oh, Dez," says Jil. And then all I hear is sobbing.

I switch on my lamp. "Jil, it's okay. Honest. Do you know how lucky I feel to have been there at all? I wouldn't trade it for anything. Jil," I plead, "stop crying. Please. I'm such a jerk!"

"Turn off the light."

"If I do, will you talk to me?"

"About what?" Jil is lying with her back to me, her arms over her head as if she's protecting herself from someone swinging a baseball bat.

"About everything!" I shout.

"Fine," Jil answers flatly. "Just turn off the light."

So, I do. And for the next hour, we talk about everything I've wanted to talk about since the day she met her mother. She even confesses that her parents *were* hurt.

"Seeing them upset," says Jil, "it killed me. But Dez, ever since I can remember, I've had this dream that my real mother is my fairy godmother. She has wings that I can see through, and she's wearing a dress with soft fabric that floats around her like a cloud. And she fixes all my problems."

I'm picturing Mrs. Lewis, but I know Jil is imagining someone else.

"Then I wake up," Jil continues, "and I know how stupid that is. Only I can't stop myself from dreaming it. "But I have this wide-awake dream, too."

I hear her nestling back under the covers.

"Have you ever had someone tell you that you look exactly like their brother's friend in Cincinnati or somewhere?"

"Yeah," I answer. "My aunt Mary says I look just like the girl who lives three doors down from her. And once, when I was going into a movie, somebody kept calling me Ginger, and—"

"Exactly," says Jil. "Well, I swear, it happens to me all the time. And every time, I wonder if I'm related to that person, or if I have a twin or a sister. And now I know."

"Are you glad you know?" I ask, hoping she won't cry again.

"Yes. Definitely."

I wish I could see her face to see if she's lying, but I promised I'd leave the light off.

"Even more, I've always wanted to know why she gave me away."

"Do you know now?" I ask softly.

"Yeah. Because she had to. I mean, she was having a

baby, and my dad wanted to marry her, but she didn't love him. She thought she did, but when it came down to living with him forever, and raising a family, she just knew it wouldn't work. And besides, she was only seventeen."

"She said giving me up was the hardest thing she's ever done in her whole life. And every day since, she's wanted to meet me, and tell me she loves me. But what really got to her were the pictures of me that Mom and Dad sent every year. They started looking more and more like Penny, and she wanted Penny to know she had a sister."

Something about that hits me wrong, but I decide I'm just being a spoiled brat about the missing T-shirt, so I shut up.

"She remembers kissing me in the hospital, and wanting the best of everything in the whole world for me, and she knew she couldn't give it to me. She didn't have a job. And she wanted to finish high school."

"Did you tell her that you *do* have the best of everything? I mean, great parents and all."

"Yeah."

"Did that make her feel better?"

"Yeah. I guess. I don't know. Maybe. Anyway, she said she'd promised my parents—no contact. Not until I was eighteen."

"So what made her change her mind?"

"*Oprah.*"

"Oprah!" I shrieked.

"Yeah." Jil giggled. "She saw some show where this adopted kid got reunited with her birth mother and everybody cried, kissed and hugged, and lived happily ever after. And Mom said, 'If she can do it, so can I,' and so she started calling Mom and Dad and bugging them."

I'm picturing poor Mr. and Mrs. Lewis. I'm also thinking how confusing it is that Jil just said "mom" twice in the same sentence and meant two different people.

"Dez!" Jil says emphatically. "Stop freaking out. It's okay. Mom and Dad keep acting all worried, too. They're afraid I'll get hurt, but this is a good thing. Honest. I'm happy. I love knowing who my mother is, and who my sister is, and that if my children end up being allergic to cantaloupe, I'll know why, and—"

"Jane's allergic to cantaloupe?"

"Yeah."

"Cantaloupe?" I repeat.

"Yeah."

"What happens when she eats it?" I'm picturing Jane eating a piece of orange melon, then suddenly scratching her arms in an all-out frenzy. Or scratching her throat like mad. Would she claw at her throat? Or her arms?

"It makes her throat swell up," says Jil.

"No kidding?" Then I think about that. "You mean, she could stop getting air?"

"I don't know. I guess. I hadn't thought . . ."

Jil stops talking. Suddenly I know that she's picturing her own imaginary children not breathing.

"I bet your kids won't inherit that," I say.

"Really?"

"Sure. I mean, you eat cantaloupe, right?"

"Yeah."

"Well, there you go."

For a minute or two, nobody says anything. I turn over in bed and sink my head into the pillow. It must be after one o'clock in the morning. Suddenly, I'm so sleepy. I wish we didn't have to go to school tomorrow. I bet Jane lets Penny sleep in. I bet she writes her a note.

Dear Teacher: Please excuse Penny from school today. She ate cantaloupe and can't breathe.

A total lie, but for a good cause.

Would my parents lie for me?

I doubt it.

Is there a difference between a mom and a parent?

"Jil?"

"Yeah?"

"You're happy?"

"Yeah."

"You sure?"

"Totally."

"It . . . seems messy to me."

"Messy?"

"Yeah. You know. Two moms. They have the same name. Don't you—"

"Dez."

"Yeah?"

"I know who I am now."

I lie in the dark and think about that. Jil knows who she is. She is the biological daughter of Jane. The sister of Penny. The child of Mr. and Mrs. Lewis. Her children may or may not be allergic to cantaloupe.

I hear her, but I still don't get it.

What about me? I don't look like my parents. Okay, I'm tall like my dad, and sturdy like my mom. But that's it.

They're messy. I'm neat.

Dad likes poetry. I like verse.

Mom likes weather and swamps. I like grand pianos.

Who am *I*?

Chapter Thirteen

"'Hark, all you ladies that do sleep.'"

Dad's voice creeps into my dream.

"'The fairy queen Proserpina bids you awake and pity them that weep.'"

Oh, no. It's not a dream.

"Please, Mr. Carter," Jil moans from the twin bed next to mine. "Don't make us get up."

I roll over and stare. Just as I feared, it's not the fairy queen Proserpina. It's Dad, and he's wearing his old, yellowed terry cloth bathrobe and gross-green bedroom slippers. "Go away," I whisper, closing my eyes.

"'Golden slumbers kiss your eyes, smiles awake you when you rise.'"

I open one eye. Sure enough. He's smiling, just like his poem promised.

"Dad. If I get up, will you stop rhyming?"

"Certainly."

"Thank you."

I roll over and cover my head with my pillow. But I can still hear him.

"Your mother and I knew it was a mistake to let you girls go to that game on a school night."

That game. I wonder if he even knows who won.

Somehow, Jil and I get up. And somehow, we drag ourselves through the school day. I can only hope that none of my teachers said anything that will ever show up on a test.

And somehow, I get through the next four months, February to May. With more sleep, but not a lot worth telling about.

The most exciting thing that happens in that entire time is Mom's discovery of a rare spotted newt in one of her ponds. I try to share her joy, but honestly, it's not even a cute newt. Just slimy.

The most embarrassing thing that happens is when Mrs. Macon gives me back a C on my Warren G. Harding poem. With red pen, in her tiny, pinched hand-writing, she claims I didn't include enough facts.

Facts! In a poem! Even I know that's insane.

Dad's reaction? You can probably guess. He goes 100 percent ballistic and publicly champions a major campaign to get her fired. Privately he rants about how he'd like to see her head and hands locked up in one of those wooden torture stocks that seventeenth-century people were put in to punish them. And, as if that's not enough, he lobbies to require a poetry appreciation course for every eighth-grade teacher in the state, even if all they teach is P.E.

A bunch of administrators deal with it, and no doubt have lots of good laughs about my father, the peculiar professor-poet-parent. Lucky for me, no kids find out.

The most fun thing that happens is my very own, self-taught, sixty-day course in Fake Piano Playing. I discover an article on the Internet that explains how movie stars make it look as if they really *are* playing the piano when, in fact, they don't have a clue about music. I rent a video clip of Vladimir Horowitz playing for real, and then I imitate him. His rhythm, fingers, posture, everything. The most amazing thing I notice is that his fingers never leave the keys.

Of course, real actors have real pianos to pretend their fake music on, and I don't. So I get a big piece of poster board and draw black-and-white piano keys on it—to scale. It takes me hours to get it right. Then I sit in the den at home, playing fake piano in time to the real music streaming in from my headphones. I may look stupid, but it makes me feel like a pro.

Mom's response is to pat me on the head on her way to turn on *Local on the 8's*, saying, "Practice makes perfect."

Dad strolls through, stops, stares, and mutters, "*'Have we eaten on the insane root that takes the reason prisoner?'*"

Denver dances and twirls in time to the tunes that no one can hear but me, and says, "Dez hears secrets."

Best of all, I still get to play for-real piano, twice a week, at the Lewises'. Which is great, except that lately,

Mrs. Lewis seems smaller, as if someone has let a little of the air out of a beautiful balloon. And Mr. Lewis is quieter. As if someone cast a sadness spell over him.

The most frustrating thing that happens in all that time is that Jil never gets our shirt back from Penny, *and* she stops talking to me about it. She still goes to visit almost every weekend, but they always hand her some radically lame excuse like, "It's dirty. We'll wash it, and give it to you next time." I can tell it embarrasses Jil to even repeat this stuff, so I stop asking about the shirt.

And as hard as I try to hide it, I also know Jil can sense that I don't much like Jane and Penny anymore.

So. Overall, my life is mostly on hold. Not much to do until I get Jil back, or a piano, whichever comes first. Or ever.

At least I get out of town twice, even if it's only in my imagination. Once to Venice, Italy, when I read *The Thief Lord*—a very cool adventure about parentless kids living on their own in an amazing city of water and canals. They make a home for themselves in an abandoned movie theater and outsmart all kinds of grown-ups.

My second imaginary trip is to Israel, when I read *Samir and Yonatan*. That book makes me sad, though, because it's about a Palestinian boy stuck living with his enemies in an Israeli hospital. Sometimes I feel like that—not that my parents are enemies exactly, but they sure do seem foreign sometimes. The good thing is that Samir makes a best friend. The bad thing is that I seem to be losing mine.

The most potentially stupendous thing that happens is my how-to-get-a-piano idea. I think it up one day when Mom is moaning about the cost of summer day care for Denver.

"Sometimes I wonder if there's even any point in my working," she tells Dad, who is busy gathering up a wad of exam papers and stuffing them into his briefcase.

Denver is zooming a big plastic truck back and forth across our already scratched-up coffee table.

Mom sighs. "So much of my salary goes to pay for day care."

"Of course it's worth it," says Dad, trying to fasten the clasp, but there are too many papers sticking out. His briefcase looks like Graham's locker. "You love your work," Dad adds, glancing distractedly around the den.

"*Vroom! Vroom!*" goes Denver.

"I'll look after him," I announce.

Mom laughs.

"*Sooooper Truuuck!*" shouts Denver in a sing-songy way. His truck goes sailing off the table and crashes into a lamp.

"Denver!" yells my mother. "How many times do I have to tell you—?"

"Sorry," whispers Denver, his body shrinking so pitifully that it's incredibly cute.

"Where're my car keys?" asks Dad, picking up a stack of old magazines and looking under them.

"No, really. I will," I say.

"Will what?" asks Mom.

"Look after him," I repeat. "It'll be my summer job. And with the money you save, we can rent a piano. Maybe even buy one."

I happen to know that day care costs a lot.

"You're too young for a summer job," says Mom.

"I'm not too young to babysit. All my friends do it. Michelle. Samantha—"

"Not all day, every day."

"But this would be different. This is my home. And Denver is family."

"Frenetic family," says Mom.

"Frenetic?"

"Frenzied," says Mom. "As in, wild. Without an intermission. No rest for the weary."

"'Double, double, toil and trouble,'" says Dad, picking up an old pair of tennis shoes and shaking them upside down.

"I can read him the poems he loves," I proclaim. "All day. Every day."

Dad stops searching for his car keys and focuses on me, as if he's seeing me for the first time ever.

"At least give me a chance," I beg. "Let me look after him the first week that school's out. Just let me try. Please."

Mom looks at Dad. Dad looks at Mom. For both of them, it's that knowing look, the smug one that parents use on little kids when they agree to let them do something everyone knows is impossible. As in, sure, you can walk to Florida and join the circus. We'll help you pack. Meanwhile, we'll wait two miles down the road to drive you home because we know you'll quit.

Dad gets down on his hands and knees and looks under the sofa. He pulls out seven Legos, a tangled wad of fishing line, one chewed-up sock from when we used to have a dog, and a cereal bowl with furry lumps of blue mold growing on what might have once been milk.

"I think we should let her do it," he says quietly into the scary cave under our couch.

"*Yes!*" I scream, and dive directly onto Dad's back to give him the biggest hug ever.

"*Oomph!*" His breath bursts out in one big whoosh. He almost collapses under me.

"Sorry." With my arms still wrapped around Dad, I look up at Mom. Expectantly. Pleadingly.

She shrugs and says, "Fine." Then, in a voice filled with serious doubt, she shakes her head and adds, "I guess you just can't learn that fire is hot until you touch it."

"Yes!" I shriek, clambering off Dad's back.

He pulls himself to standing and returns my hug. I'm pretty sure he's winking at Mom over my shoulder.

Who cares?

I run to thank Mom next. She gives me a loving squeeze, but it's the kind with sadness in it—the kind that whispers, *I hate to see you fail, but life is all about trying.*

I know they're setting me up for defeat, but I'll show them.

Chapter Fourteen

Today is the last day of eighth grade. I can't wait until tomorrow.

Tomorrow is when I start Denver duty. Full time.

I'm cleaning out my locker when Graham strolls by. He stops and says, "You gotta be kidding."

"Huh?" I look up at him. He is cute. But his shirt is buttoned lopsided because he must have matched the buttons wrong, and now one side is three inches longer than the other.

"That's your locker?" he asks, squinting.

"Uh-huh. Why?"

"It looks like the inside of a . . . of a . . . ," he stammers, and gives up. "I can't think of anything to compare it to." He leans into the open door. "I've never seen anything so neat." He backs away. "Except maybe Jil's kitchen."

"Yeah, well. I lugged most of my stuff home yesterday," I lie.

"Oh. Okay." He seems relieved.

That's when I notice that he's holding a big black trash bag full of something. He lifts it up and explains.

"Useless accumulations of eighth grade. On its way to the first Dumpster I find."

I stifle a desperate urge to grab it and go through every grimy sock and gum wrapper. There's bound to be some good stuff in there somewhere. What if he's throwing away his watch, an unused notebook, or a perfectly good pen?

"Seen Jil?" he attempts to ask casually.

"Yeah. Some." I shove the neat stack of books on my top shelf into a heap so it'll look less perfect.

"She still going to visit her real family all the time?"

It's all I can do not to yell that the Lewises *are* her real family! Instead, I say, "Beginning tomorrow, she's spending the whole month of June with them."

"Wow."

"Yeah."

"Well, see you around, Dez."

"Yeah. You, too, Graham. Have a fun summer."

I watch him trudge down the hall, dragging his trash bag behind him. Poor guy. It's been five months since she dumped him. And he's still asking about her. Well, he's got all summer. That ought to do it.

"Good luck," I whisper as he vanishes around the corner.

I straighten the pushed-over pile of books and slide them into my backpack. Then I pull out a handful of pens that are held together by a rubber band, and zip them into the see-through outside pocket of my backpack.

All that's left for me to do is return a library book and

then find Mr. Trimble. I want to thank him for the reading suggestions he gave me.

After I leave the library, I find him in his classroom, all bent over, lowering stacks of books into a big cardboard box.

"Hey, thanks, Mr. Trimble," I say. "You put me onto some very cool imaginary travel this year."

He straightens up, arching his back like it hurts, but his face is filled with pure joy. He's flashing me a grin so huge you'd think I'd just informed him that his whole life was worthwhile and now he could die happy.

"So tell me. Where did all that reading take you?"

"Lots of places. Africa. Israel. Italy."

"No kidding? That's great. What's next?"

"China," I answer, but I'm making that up. I doubt I'll do any reading this summer, with Denver to look after. Except for maybe a million or two trips to Whoville. Denver loves Dr. Seuss.

"Well. Have a great summer!" I wave and back out the door before he can ask me to name the China book.

Whump.

I plow straight into Mrs. Macon on her way down the hall. The last person in the entire world I want to see.

Look down and keep walking, I tell myself.

"Dez." Her lips are as pinched and tight as her handwriting. "I do hope you have an interesting summer planned."

Obviously, she doesn't mean that. Not that I blame her. After all, my dad tried to get her fired.

"Thanks," I mumble. "I'm babysitting my brother. Every day."

"That's nice." She turns to leave.

"Uh . . . Mrs. Macon, I'm sorry about all the trouble my dad caused you." I figure it's the least I can say.

She swings back around to me. Slowly. "You should be proud of your dad."

"Excuse me?"

"He has things he's passionate about, Dez. Like poetry." She pauses, stares out somewhere over my head, and coughs up a nervous little laugh. "*I'm* passionate about the presidents, you know." Then she heaves a long, deep sigh, and adds, "But I can't fault anyone for doing what he thinks is right."

"Well, yeah. For sure," I answer. "And that's, uh, nice of you to say so. Especially, uh—" I falter. She *is* being nice, right?

"Give him my best." She dismisses me with one of those cheery bye-bye-for-now hand gestures.

"Yeah. Sure. I will."

I watch her disappear down the hall.

Go figure.

But then I remember that I have more important things to do than try and understand a teacher who may be even weirder than my dad.

So, good-bye, Mrs. Macon. Good-bye, eighth grade.

Hello, Denver duty.

Chapter Fifteen

7:00 A.M.
My alarm goes off.
"Dez-Dez-Dez! Dez-Dez-Dez!"
Over and over. "Dez-Dez-Dez!" I cover my head with my pillow. There it goes again. Muted, but relentless. "Dez-Dez-Dez!"

My alarm is a small, very loud three-year-old boy named Denver, wearing dinosaurs on his feet.

7:01 A.M.
I groan.

7:04 A.M.
I get up.

7:05 A.M.
I start to make my bed, but Denver needs to go to the bathroom and he wants me to accompany him. On the way there, he remembers that his plastic pig won't go oink anymore, so we look for a new battery.

7:14 A.M.

We're still looking for a battery.

7:15 A.M.

Denver wets his *Frog and Toad* pajamas.

7:16 A.M.

I sponge up wee-wee. Change Denver's clothes. Put his pajamas in the washing machine. Look for carpet shampoo.

7:25 A.M.

No carpet shampoo. I decide to cook him breakfast. No eggs. No milk. I mix dry cereal with some blueberries, give Denver a spoon, and place him in front of the TV. I find *Dragon Tales* for him, but he wants to watch the Weather Channel. I stifle a scream.

7:28 A.M.

I try to wipe up blueberry stains, which can't be done, so I search, one more time, for carpet shampoo.

7:34 A.M.

I look for Band-Aids. How can anyone cut his toe on a spoon? Eventually, I find a Big Bird Band-Aid in the drawer with the telephone book, but Denver wants a *Frog and Toad* Band-Aid. He is very into *Frog and Toad*.

7:45 A.M.

I decide to *read* him *Frog and Toad*, hoping that will make up for no Band-Aid.

8:32 A.M.

We are still reading, and rereading, *Frog and Toad*. It's a good thing I like these stories.

8:33 A.M.

Denver needs to go to the bathroom. Number two. This time he wants to go by himself. I say, "No. You need help when you wipe." He screams, "I can do it!" and shuts the bathroom door in my face. It locks.

8:34 A.M.

Mom calls out, "I'm off to work, Dez. Call me if you need me." I yell back, "I can do it!"

I try not to cry.

8:38 A.M.

I find a knife and pop the lock. The good news is that Denver has not gone number two yet. The bad news is that he flushed his plastic pig down the toilet and stopped it up. Water is running over the commode basin and covering the floor.

8:39 A.M.

Dad knocks on the bathroom door. "I'm leaving now. You guys okay in there?"

8:40 A.M.

"We're fine," I answer. "Have a good day." Denver shouts, "We're swimming!" I cover his mouth to shut him up.

8:41 to 11:48 A.M.

I unstop the toilet, help Denver go number two, mop the floor, put his *Frog and Toad* pajamas in the dryer, read him four books, work seven puzzles, take his pajamas out of the dryer, go for a walk, wash the mud out of his hair, fix him a snack, remember that I never ate breakfast, fix myself a snack, play Go Fish, teach him his numbers, let him fill the kitchen sink with bubbles and throw toys into it, make a megaphone out of a cardboard paper-towel tube, answer the phone, tell the telemarketer we don't want any, find Denver, glue the broken picture frame back together, wonder what Jil is doing at Jane's house, wonder if I really want a piano bad enough to do this for an entire summer, wonder if I can even do it for one whole day.

11:49 a.m. to 12:03 P.M.
Lunch.

12:04 to 2:29 P.M.

I make a bet with Denver that he can't sit on a basketball and bounce for thirty minutes. I make a bet with Denver that he can't run up and down the driveway for twenty minutes. I reward Denver for winning both bets by making him slice-n-bake chocolate chip cookies. I wash the cookie sheet. Scrub melted chocolate out of the carpet. Add milk, eggs, and carpet shampoo to the grocery list. Answer the telephone and tell Dad we're fine. Answer the phone and tell Mom we're fine. Find Denver. Make him put all the silverware back in the drawer.

2:30 P.M.
Naptime. Both of us.

4:00 P.M.
Talk Denver into watching a two-hour movie with me.

4:20 P.M.
Turn off the movie. Bet Denver that he can't put all his puzzles together without my help.

4:25 P.M.
Help Denver put all his puzzles back together.

4:45 P.M.
Mom comes home.

"You're early!" I cry out, trying to hide my joy.

"I thought you might be climbing the walls," she says. At the same time, I know she's eyeing me for telltale signs of defeat, exhaustion, or serious blood loss.

"I'm fine," I say, radiating total success.

"Really?" She seems stunned.

"Yep. We had fun, didn't we, Denver?"

"Uh-huh." He nods like a bobble-head. "Mom"—he tugs on her hand—"can Dez day-care me tomorrow?"

Mom looks from cheerful me to happy Denver. "You're really serious about this piano, aren't you?"

Well, duh.

"Yes," I answer.

Mom tilts her head and studies me. "I just never thought it would last. You know?"

"Yeah, Mom. I know. But it has lasted. It's lasted almost six months, and I can look after Denver for two and a half more. No problem." I hope I sound more confident than I feel right now.

"Destiny," she says. "I'm proud of you. You're growing up."

I grin all the way to my room, where I collapse onto my unmade bed. I can't believe it's five o'clock in the afternoon and I haven't made my bed yet. Even more amazing, I'm not going to make it now, either. I plan to be back in it by seven. Maybe sooner. Even with the nap, I feel like I've just paddled a canoe fifty miles—upstream. How am I going to do this? No wonder day-care people charge a fortune.

But then I remember, they do it every day. It must be a conditioning thing. Like training to run a marathon. The first day you can barely run two miles, but after a month of training, ten miles is nothing.

Heck. By the end of June, I'll be able to start my own day care. With ten kids. Maybe twenty. I punch my fist into the air. Bring 'em on!

But the very best thing is that, finally, Mom is getting it. Dad will, too.

The phone rings and I roll over and check out the Caller ID. It says *Jil Lewis*. That's her cell phone. She must be calling from Mom-2's house.

"Hi," I say, so excited to hear from her.

"Dez," she says. *"You've gotta help me."*

She's crying.

Chapter Sixteen

il." I grip the phone so tightly my knuckles turn white. "What's wrong?"

"I hate her!" Jil sobs.

"Who?"

"Mom!"

"Mom-2?"

"Yeah."

"What happened?"

"D-Dez." Jil's voice catches, making the word sound more like a hiccup than a name. "You've got to help me. You've got to come help me."

"Where are you?"

"Greensboro."

"Jane's house?"

"Yeah." More hiccup sounds. More sobs.

"Jil! Get a grip. Tell me what's happened. I can't help you unless you tell me what's happened."

Then there's a long silence. Except for sobs and hiccups, I hear nothing.

Finally, Jil says, "I need you to come to Greensboro."

She sounds more like herself, but stretched tight, as if she's pulling everything together just to get these words out.

"Jil. Greensboro is sixty miles from here. How am I supposed to get there?"

"You can take a bus. Tomorrow. I've already checked the schedule. One leaves at—"

"I can't." My mind is racing. Zooming ahead of itself. "I've got to look after Denver tomorrow," I say. That's my autopilot answer, but my brain is still trying to work out why Jil is crying. Why she needs me to take a bus to Greensboro.

"He can go to day care."

"No," I say. "He can't. My parents have cancelled day care for the summer. They're counting on me. I can't cancel, Jil. I'm doing this to get a piano."

"A piano!" Jil shrieks. She starts crying again. I wait.

Finally, she gets herself together again, and says in a controlled voice that sounds like her teeth are clenched, "Dez. This is more important than a piano. You can have my piano."

"Why? Jil, why is this more important? I can't help you if you don't tell me."

"I got arrested."

Suddenly the telephone feels like a brick. I can't believe what I just heard. "You what?"

"Arrested. Put in jail. Cuffed."

"You did not."

"Okay. Not cuffed. And not in jail like a cell. But we did get arrested. Me and Penny. We got pushed around and treated like criminals, and hauled into a security room at the shopping center." Suddenly her voice grows louder. "And I mean hauled, Dez. Not escorted. Not taken. *Hauled*. Like delinquents. Like crooks. Like crud."

"Who did that?"

"The security guy. Then he called the cops."

"Jil!" I shout into the phone. "What'd you do? You're not making any sense!"

"Penny shoplifted a necklace. From Banana Republic. And a salesperson saw her do it. But the security guy dragged me along with Penny because I was older and he thought I made her do it, but I didn't. And Penny even told him I didn't, but he didn't believe her, at first. But later, after the cops came, he did."

Words are firing out of Jil like bullets.

"And Jane came to rescue us, but she . . . she . . . didn't . . . I mean . . . not me . . . see— "

Jil is crying again and can't talk. I wait.

"Jane thought I did it. No way her precious Penny could have done it. And she wanted the cops to take me to jail. She only wanted to take Penny home. Just her. Not me. She was so mad. You should have seen her. But they don't really arrest ten-year-olds, or thirteen-year-olds, either, if they've never done anything wrong, which I haven't. They just needed a parent to come pick us up. Later we'll have to see a guidance counselor or a shrink

or another cop or something. I don't know, but whatever
. . . the police sent me home with Jane."

For the second time today, I feel exhausted. Like I've
paddled fifty miles again. "Where are you now?"

"At Mom's. Mom-2's. You were right. 'Mom-2' is a
great name for her. But I'm leaving."

"Good. Are your parents coming to get you?"

"Dez. You're not listening. I'm leaving. I hate her. But
I'm not going home. I can't. My parents think I'm going
to be here a whole month, and I can't tell them about
this. I just can't."

Uh-oh. I don't even want to know what she thinks
she's going to do next. So I don't say a word.

"Dez? You still there?"

"No."

"Come on, Dez. I've got a plan. I need you here. But
don't tell your parents why. Promise me you won't. Just
ask them if you can come spend the month with me,
and—"

"The month! Are you crazy?"

"Promise you won't tell."

"Okay, fine, I won't tell, but—"

"I've got credit cards. I have a cell phone. I can get
money from ATMs. We can stay in a hotel. Swim in their
pool. Go to the mall every day. Dez, it will be so cool—"

"You're crazy. You know that?"

"Well. Okay. Maybe not for a month, but until I figure
out what to tell my parents."

"Jil. Stay with Jane. I bet she'll apologize. Give it a day."

"She already did. She even cried. Said she was sorry. Said she loved me. But it's just no good anymore. I'm not sure it was ever any good."

"This is so awful. I mean . . . terrible. Devastating. The worst. But Jil, give it a day. Okay? Please? You'll feel different tomorrow. Maybe not better, but different? All right?"

"You mean you won't come?"

There's a roaring noise in my head that's louder than Niagara Falls. What am I supposed to say? What's the matter with her? Live in Greensboro? In a hotel? For a month? Give up the only chance I'll ever have to own a piano?

"Jil," I say softly. "We're not old enough to rent a room."

"I need you. Are you coming or not?"

"Listen to me. Stay at Jane's. Please. Just for tonight. Call me in the morning—"

"Will you come, Dez? Just answer me. Yes . . . or no?"

I think about it. I take a deep breath. I close my eyes. I answer her.

"No."

Chapter Seventeen

I am totally wiped out with exhaustion, but there is no way I'm going to sleep.

I jump up from my still unmade bed, and pace. Three steps to my bookshelf. *Arrested! Jil got arrested!* Two steps to my desk. *Penny swiped a necklace.* Five steps to my closet. *Her mother is a snake. A skunk. A creep.* Seven steps—between both beds—to my bedside table. *Poor Jil. She really does need me. Big-time.*

I sit down on the bed. *A bus to Greensboro! Live in a hotel! No way!* I stand up. *No piano!* Eight steps back to my desk. I straighten the tilted lampshade. *Forget the piano.* Five steps to the closet. *I can't forget it. I've got to babysit Denver. Mom and Dad are counting on me.* Six steps to the bookshelf. *Jil's counting on me too. I mean, no way I'm going to live in a hotel, but shouldn't I go help her get through this?* I kick the bookshelf. *No. I had to say no.* Three steps back to the bed. *Whoa! What about the last time I said no? When I thought I was doing the right thing. Saving her from a psycho. And then Jane turned out to be nice. And everybody lived happily ever after.* I lean forward and stack three CDs so that the edges line up perfectly. *But she isn't so nice after all, is she? And happily ever after is nothing but a fairy tale.*

I sit down on my bed again, slumped, one leg straight, one bent, studying my feet. *My big, brave, just-say-no— it didn't matter then. Why should it matter now?*

I pick up the phone to call her back. *At least talk to her. Keep her occupied for a while. Until she feels better.*

I jump back up. *No. I don't want to hear the convincing Christopher Columbus voice. By tomorrow she'll be over it. No big deal. Get some sleep. Denver duty tomorrow.*

I plop back down. *Denver duty. Another fifty miles. Upstream.* I curl up in a ball and groan.

I stare at my clock.

Go to sleep.

No way.

10:45 P.M. I'm still staring at my clock. *Didn't Mrs. Macon say people should be respected for doing what they think is right?*

Midnight. Still staring at my clock. *Wouldn't that include people like terrorists?*

3:00 A.M. Staring at my clock. *Who the heck gets to decide what right is, anyway?*

4:00 A.M. Still staring at the stupid clock.

7:00 A.M.

"Dez-Dez-Dez! Dez-Dez-Dez!"

Nooooooo.

❀

Denver-wise, today goes better. He breaks only two things—a dinner plate that was chipped anyway and a clay pot that I'm guessing no one will ever miss. That's because the plant that was shriveled up in it didn't look as if it had been watered in my lifetime.

No cut toes. No bathroom accidents. The only important thing he ruins is my fake piano keyboard, which is totally trashed by a Denver creativity attack—one blue crayon, one brown. Yesterday, that would have sent me into orbit. Today it seems trivial.

I am so worried about Jil.

While Denver eats breakfast, I dial her cell phone. Mom brought home eggs yesterday, so I make him egg-in-a-hole—an egg fried in a piece of buttered bread with a circle cut in the middle.

All I get is, "Hey. This is Jil. Leave a message and I'll call you back."

I leave a message that says, "Call me. Please."

But she doesn't.

During the course of the day, I call, I don't know, fifty times, maybe. I leave only one more message, though. I say, "Hey. I am so worried about you. Call me. I'm sorry I said I wouldn't come to Greensboro. Maybe I will come. For the day or something. Just call me. I need to talk to you. Please."

By afternoon, I've frantically punched in her number so many times that three times I get wrong numbers.

One time I get that stupid recording that says, "If you'd like to make a call, hang up and try again. If you need help—"

"I don't need help!" I scream into the phone. "Jil needs help!" I slam it back into its holder.

Denver gapes at me, mouth wide open, and then he shrieks.

I hurry over to hug him. "It's okay," I say, holding him close and smoothing his silky blond hair with one hand.

His hair is nothing like mine. Lighter, finer. Mine is dark brown and thick. We look nothing alike. Penny and Jil look exactly alike.

"You scared me," he whimpers.

"I'm sorry, Denver." I snuggle my neck over the curve of his head. "Let's do something fun. You want to play in the sprinkler?"

"Yes!" he shrieks, shooting straight up like a missile. His head smacks my jaw like a hammer. The first thing that registers is the pain. The second thing is the salty taste of the blood that's pouring from the tongue I just bit.

"Sorry, Dez. Sorry, Dez. Sorry, Dez." Each time he says it, he shrinks smaller.

"'S'okay," I reassure him, my cupped hand catching most of the blood.

By the time Dad gets home, I've stopped bleeding, but Denver has played in the sprinkler so long he could pass for a prune.

"And how are swift runner Achilles and the beautiful fairy queen?" greets Dad.

"*Peachy,*" I answer, and bolt straight for my room. I grab my telephone and dial Jil's cell number one more time.

"Hey. This is Jil. Leave a message and I'll call you back."

I click off the familiar message and dial Information, speaking clearly to the recording. "Greensboro. North Carolina. Jane Simons. Um . . . er . . . Simmons." Is her name Simmons or Simons? I can't remember. My stuttering brings the operator on.

"Would you please look up both names?" I ask.

"I have a J. Simmons on Dellwood Drive."

Quickly, I dial the number she gives me. After three rings, a voice that sounds like Mom-2's answers.

Oh, great! What do I call her? Jane? Mrs. Simons? Or was it Simmons?

"Hi . . . um . . . This is Dez Carter. May I speak to Jil?"

"Dez! How are you?" Mom-2 sounds totally pleasant. "Jil isn't here, honey. Her dad picked her up early this morning."

I'm so thankful to hear that, I almost hang up on her. "Thanks, Mrs. . . . uh . . . thanks! I'll try her at home."

"How's your summer going, dear?"

My summer? All two days of it? What's with this woman, sounding like life is all lovely when we both know it's not?

"Just fine, thanks. Bye." I hang up before she can tell me how terrific Penny's summer is going.

Relieved, I dial the Lewises.

"Mrs. Lewis." I actually heave a sigh into the receiver.

"Dez!" Her greeting is warm, and I can tell she's genuinely happy to hear from me. None of that fakey, how's-your-summer-honey? garbage.

"Hi, Mrs. Lewis. Can I speak to Jil, please?"

There's silence. Uh-oh. Maybe Jil's in so much trouble she's not allowed to come to the phone. Maybe that's why she didn't return my messages. But wait, Jil didn't steal anything. Penny did. What's she told her parents?

Mrs. Lewis, her voice in kind of a fog, finally says, "Jil's in Greensboro with Jane, Dez. All month. I thought you knew that."

"Uh . . . yeah . . . of course. I guess I forgot. Is . . . is . . . Mr. Lewis home?"

"Well, yes, Dez. He is. Would you like to speak to him?"

"Oh. Well, no. I mean, thanks, but never mind."

I hang up, knowing she thinks I'm a nutcase. But that is only one tiny reason that my stomach has just turned ten somersaults. And my face has flamed up like a furnace.

Where is Jil?

My fingers are already dialing Michelle Redmon's number.

"Michelle," I gasp into the phone. "I need a huge

favor. Can you babysit Denver for me tomorrow?"

"Denver?" she asks, clearly incredulous. "All day?"

"I'll pay you double! Please. It's an emergency."

"Okay, Dez. Sure. I can handle—"

"Thanks!" I practically shriek into the phone. My head's spinning with a million details that don't fit yet. But they will. I'll make them. When's the bus leave? How'm I going to do this?

"Michelle, come at nine tomorrow morning. Okay?"

I hang up and flop back onto my bed. My head hits the pillow—a muffled explosion of feathers.

What am I doing?

Chapter Eighteen

Okay. So maybe I panicked.

In the heat of the moment, all I could think of was Jil hanging out by herself in some sleazy motel. Having gone from two moms to none. Overnight.

So I called Michelle to babysit Denver for me, so that I can . . . can . . . do what? Take a sleazy bus by *my*self? All the way to Greensboro? *Are* buses sleazy? I've never ridden one. They're safe. Aren't they?

Then what? Am I clairvoyant? Telepathic? I think not. I think I don't have a clue where to find Jil.

Basically, I'm just trying very hard to think straight. But my brain won't cooperate.

Eventually, I regroup enough to realize that Jil is definitely listening to my messages. I know her. She's just not returning them. Because she knows how to scare me into doing exactly what she wants. Or, she's been kidnapped. I'm praying it's the first one.

So if leave a new message telling her I'm coming, she'll get it. She can meet me at the bus station. Then I'll talk her into coming back.

That'll work. Won't it?

So, do I let Mom and Dad leave for work tomorrow thinking I'm staying with Denver? Then slip Michelle in as a sub for the day? Can I get back before they get home? What's the bus schedule?

Dez, you idiot! Denver can talk, you know. He's three years old, not one. Don't you think he just might notice that Michelle is too short to be his sister? Don't you also think he just might mention that to Mom?

Besides, that is so dishonest, it hurts to even think about it. I can't believe I did think about it.

I pace back and forth again—desk to bed to closet to bookshelf—over and over. Sometimes I stop at the window and look out, thinking of a million possibilities that won't work.

Tell my parents. *That's* the plan that'll work. But Jil made me swear not to. Besides, if I show up with a parent, she'll lay low. She'll split. I know she will. And end up who knows where?

It's got to be just me.

And I need a good story. One that's so convincing they won't trash my chance for a piano. Suddenly, I wish I had a Christopher Columbus voice. I don't have nearly enough experience for this.

I check the bus schedule.

I make up my story.

Then I go looking for Dad.

He's in his study, elbows propped on his desk. Papers piled everywhere. Cigarette butts stacked up in tiny, disposable aluminum ashtrays, looking like a bunch of tiny toxic pyramids. Dad smokes like he's got a death wish.

From the den, I hear "Heat index . . . Doppler radar . . . Bermuda high . . . evening storms . . . variable clouds," accompanied by obnoxious music. Mom's home, too.

Denver's curled up next to her on the sofa, clutching a blanket. How come he never sat still on my shift?

I suck in a deep breath.

Who do I talk to about this? Mom or Dad? I let the air back out of my lungs slowly, thinking.

Dad looks super-involved in the papers he's hunched over. Mom is in weather land.

I stand in the hall between them both and blurt, "Can I go to Greensboro tomorrow to visit Jil?"

Dad doesn't hear me, but Mom raises herself up on one elbow, stares at me in disbelief, and says, "Can you *what*?"

She turns down the TV.

"I know I said I'd keep Denver all summer," I explain quickly, rushing into the room. "And I will. But Jil wants me to come see her tomorrow. Just for the day. There's this very cool all-day thing at the university there, kind of a day camp for eighth graders to explore painting, acting, science, you name it, and there's a special class for piano, tomorrow only, and Jil knew I would love it, so I asked Michelle if she could babysit Denver tomorrow, and she said yes, and I can take a bus that leaves at 9:30 and be back by 7:00 tomorrow night." I desperately suck in a reload of air, then add, "Doesn't that sound cool?"

It's not as if I'm a goody-goody kid who has never told her parents something that wasn't true before, but I'm not exactly a professional liar, either. And now that all those lies have spewed out of my mouth like poison, I feel sick.

Mom sits up and says, "Dez. Come here." She pats the sofa seat beside her.

When I ease down beside her, she looks at me in a way that can only be labeled *disappointment*.

"You've kept Denver for only two days." She takes my hand and strokes it like it's a naughty puppy. "I didn't expect you to make it all summer, but honestly, Dez, I thought you'd last longer than a couple of days."

"I'm not quitting!" I exclaim. "It's just for one day. Honest. I can do this. And I'm not letting you down. I got Michelle. She's great. She—"

"Dez," says Mom. "You're not taking a bus to Greens-boro—"

I jerk my hand away. "But Mom."

"Let me finish. I have a job to quote tomorrow—for a company that's based in Greensboro. I'll drop you off at Jil's mother's house, and pick you up when I'm finished."

I throw my arms around her. "Mom! Thank you! That is so—"

She pushes me back gently and says, "But we won't need for Michelle to babysit. I'll just drop Denver at day care."

"You can't," I protest. "Remember? You cancelled. You lost his place for the summer. They—"

Denver uncurls himself out from under his blanket and chants, "I want Dez-care—"

"Dez," says Mom, guiltily avoiding eye contact. "We . . . uh." She clears her throat. "We never cancelled. Your dad and I . . . we talked about it, sweetheart. We knew you'd get tired of keeping Denver. And this whole piano thing," she sighs as she reaches for the TV clicker, touching her finger to the volume control. "When push came to shove, we knew it wouldn't last."

If I'd been cracked in the head with a baseball bat, it would have hurt less.

They *never* cancelled Denver's day care! They didn't believe I could do it! Not for a week. Not for a minute.

When push comes to shove? What does that mean? Why does she talk in those ancient little sayings of hers that never make any sense? Okay. *I'll* push. *I'll* shove. Both of them. Over a cliff. And then I'll stand at the top and look down and shout Latin verbs, epic poetry, *sink or swim, all's well that ends well, you scratch my back, I'll scratch yours, rise and shine, get your ducks in a row, there's no place like home—*

Sobbing, I run from the room.

Mom follows me. "Honey," she calls after me. "For crying out loud, Dez. Get a grip on yourself!"

I want to hit her.

"What's going on?" Dad asks from out of his office coma.

Mom, right on my heels, takes a swerving detour into his office, where I can hear the hum of parent voices as I dash up the stairs to my room. Mom, no doubt explaining how I wasn't bright-eyed and bushy-tailed enough to seize the bull by the horns. Dad, probably fighting off his disillusionment in me and consoling her with some lame Shakespearean quote—"*Much ado about nothing*"?

Well, I know Shakespeare, too, you know. "'*A plague on both your houses!*'" I shout down the steps.

I march into my room and slam the door.

You know how things always seem better the next day—after you've slept on your problems? Well, it's morning now, and I swear, I'm even madder. As a matter of fact, it would be fine with me to live in another city for a month. Why not? My parents know *nothing* about me.

I'm also ten times more worried about Jil. She's still not answering, so I leave her a message to take a cab and meet me outside, in front of Elliott Hall, the building where the UNCG bookstore is. I looked up the university campus on the Internet and got directions. Then I talked Mom into dropping me there instead of Jane's house.

"It's quicker to take me straight to Elliott Hall," I explain. "That's where the Arts and Science Camp meets. Next to the bookstore. Jil's meeting me there."

I say this so convincingly that I almost believe it myself.

What if Jil isn't there? Do I call the Lewises and tell

them Jil has run away from Jane's? Do I phone the police and report a missing person? Or do I just hang out all day in the university bookstore, pretending I'm a student, waiting for Mom to come back?

All the way to Greensboro, Mom tries to make me feel better. "Every cloud has a silver lining. Besides, you're too young to spend your entire summer watching a three-year-old."

Too young is supposed to make me feel better?

"It's not healthy," she continues.

I'd like to tell her that she is two grapes short of a fruit salad, and that a house divided will not stand, but instead, I just keep my mouth shut. What's the point? I can't tell her about Jil, and she so doesn't understand a thing about me, anyway.

With the help of my navigating instructions, she turns the car onto the street that runs in front of Elliott Hall. But cars can't go all the way up to the entrance because there's a huge grassy area that stretches for almost a block in front of it.

"You can let me off here," I say.

"Where's Jil?" She cranes her neck, trying to pick her out of all the people milling around the front of the building.

"Inside," I lie.

"I don't want to leave you here until I see her."

"Mom!" I exclaim. "I'm not Denver. I'll be fourteen soon. I can find her."

Mom reaches into the backseat for her purse. Since

she's meeting clients in an office today, she has on real clothes and is carrying a pocketbook instead of her ugly, worn-out, zippered fanny pack.

"Here." She dumps a handful of quarters into my palm. "If Jil's not there, call me on my cell phone. I'll come right back for you."

"Fine."

"And Dez, honey. Enjoy your piano camp. You know I want you to have fun. If you're still interested when school starts, maybe we can work something out. Maybe—"

"I gotta go, Mom."

"We love you. You know that."

I point to my watch. "I'm going to be late."

"Do you have the money I gave you for the day? Not the change for the pay phone, but the—"

I pat the back pocket of my Capri pants. "I got it, Mom."

"Don't forget, always put your best foot forward."

"Right." I punch my thumb up in the air.

Finally, Mom pulls away. I follow the pedestrian walk to Elliott Hall, a big new building with gigantic square columns. Lots of kids who act like they know what they're doing are strolling in every direction. Some are even my age. Maybe there really is an eighth-grade summer Arts and Science Camp.

I get closer to the big glass entrance doors. The doors where I told Jil to meet me. Outside.

I turn, and spot Mom's green Subaru Forester, covered in swamp mud, still creeping down the road, trying not to turn until I give her a sign. The driver of the silver minivan behind her is honking his horn. I point to a person who could be Jil, but isn't, and wave enthusiastically at Mom.

The dark green Subaru seems to visibly perk up, happy now, and scoots around the corner.

I turn back to the tall glass doors.

Jil isn't here.

Chapter Nineteen

The University of North Carolina at Greensboro is a public university. It was chartered in 1891. The campus covers two hundred acres. The student–faculty ratio is fourteen to one. Approximately fifteen thousand students from forty-six states and ninety countries. In the last hour and ten minutes, I have personally watched half of them walk by.

There are more women than men. The men's soccer team did super last year and Jackson Library has more books than a beach has sand. There's a campus rock that, by tradition, serves as a giant message board, and cannot be repainted more often than every twenty-four hours. Today, it's painted red and says, COMEDY SHOW at 8:00, something about a party, and FREE ICE CREAM AT YUM YUM'S.

Is there anything else you'd like to know about the place where I've been sitting—hot, sweaty, and worried out of my mind—ever since Mom dropped me here forever ago?

During that time, I've learned tons about this school, because I've read every sign and brochure in sight. I can also tell you a lot about my feet. Why? Because I'm trying to choose the best one.

My mother, the cliché queen, told me to put my best foot forward, so I'm bored enough to wonder, which foot *is* best? I'm wearing sandals, so it should be easy to tell, but it's not.

My right foot is slightly bigger. Is bigger better? My mom says good things come in small packages. The second toe on my left foot is slightly crooked, but the cuticle on the third toe of my right foot is out of control. I figure it's a tie.

Where *is* Jil?

I finger the loose change in my pocket and wonder, do I call Mom, Dad, the Lewises, or the police?

Eeny, meeny, miny, mo.

"Surprise!" Jil, with her arms thrown wide, leaps out from around the corner of the building.

I have never been so happy to see anyone in my whole life. "Jil!" I screech, leaping up and running to hug her. "How are you? Where have you been? Where's Jane? Where'd you spend the night? I have been *soooo* worried!"

Jil grins. She looks a little ratty. Less than perfect. Her cute blond hair is kind of tangled, but now that I know she hasn't been kidnapped or murdered, my fear morphs directly into rage.

"What's the matter with you? Are you crazy? You've made me be a liar, a cheat, a fraud, and a . . . a . . . I don't know what else. I could kill you! You owe me. Big-time."

"Whoa." Jil pushes me back. Holding me at arm's length, a smile practically splits her face. "I'm *so* glad you're here!" She barely gets the words out before her face contorts into a twisted mess, and tears stream down her cheeks.

We hug each other like survivors of a bomb scare.

And then she shrugs me off.

"Dez," she says. "This is so cool. You just wait. We're going to have a blast. We're free! Just think! No parents! You're going to love it!"

I think, if I'm going to love it, why were you sobbing two seconds ago? But I leave it alone. For now.

"I've got the whole day figured out. Just think, thanks to you, here we are on a college campus. Brilliant! I bet there's a place close by that does body piercing. Navel?" Jil weaves her body back and forth like an exotic dancer and points to her belly button. "Eyebrow?" She twists the corner above her right eye like some sinister villain would tweak an ultrathin mustache.

I sit down on the front steps of the building and roll my eyes. That dumb idea doesn't even deserve an answer.

"But first"—she plops down next to me and continues, as though I'd just said, *Yes, please, stick a needle in my face*—"we need to check into a hotel room. I called and made us a reservation. Then we can take bubble baths and order room service. How does eggs Benedict sound?"

"Jil," I say. "One night of freedom has made you

delusional. We're too young to rent a room." The other reason, which I don't say, is that Mom is picking me up at four o'clock. I'd better wait until later to tell her that.

"You're six feet tall," she says. "You can easily pass for eighteen."

My head jerks up. Is that why she wants me here? To get her a room? "I'm five-eight, and I'm thirteen," I say flatly.

"You'll be fourteen in two weeks. You can try. Okay? The hotel is only a few blocks from here. We can walk. Please. I need to sleep in a bed."

I check out the tangled hair again. "Where *did* you spend last night?"

Jil stretches out her legs and stares at her feet for a long time. Picking the best one to put forward? I doubt it. Finally, she says, "Target."

"Target!" I shriek.

"Yeah. It's near Mom's house. They stay open twenty-four hours."

"You cruised the deodorant and pots-and-pans aisles of Target all night, and nobody noticed you were just a tiny bit out of place?"

"Well, yeah, they did notice. So, around one A.M., when one of the clerks started watching me funny, I left, then sneaked back into the bathroom and didn't come out."

I stare at Jil. She's done some weird stuff, but this beats them all. "You slept on a toilet?"

"No. I *sat* on a toilet. Sleep wasn't an option." She leans her body into mine, cozy, like we're both in on the same joke. "That's why I was late. I've been on campus for hours. Practically since dawn. Waiting on a sofa in one of the lounges, but I sort of fell asleep."

"Jil." I flop my arm over her shoulder. "Let's go home."

She slides two feet away and, through clenched teeth, says, "No way."

The next thing I know, I'm letting her push me up in front of a reservation clerk at the Sheraton. I stand up as straight as I can and chirp, "Hi! I'm Destiny Carter, and I'd like to check into my room, please."

A young woman with sophisticated pulled-back hair looks up at me and smiles. "Do you have a reservation?" she asks pleasantly.

"Yes, ma'am. I do. It's under my name, Destiny Carter."

Jil elbows me in the ribs.

I know. I elbow her back. I shouldn't have said "ma'am."

The clerk types something into her computer. Then, with her face still directed at the keyboard, she says, "May I see some identification, please."

I shoot Jil a look that says *See? I told you so*, and turn to walk away. She grabs my arm and holds me in place. "She lost her purse," Jil explains. "Can you believe it? Do you know how much trouble it is to get all your credit cards replaced, your license reissued?"

The clerk looks up, and says, sweetly, professionally, "I'm sorry, ladies, but we can't rent rooms to minors."

"She's not—"

I jerk Jil away from the counter and out of the building before she can say another word.

"We can try someplace else," she calls after me as I stomp down the street. "Hey! Wait up. I know! We can tell the clerk at the next place that there's a camera crew coming from CBS to film a reality show. You know, a show all about kids and what kinds of goofy stuff they'd do if they could stay in a hotel without their parents."

I whirl around to tell her that she is certifiably insane, only to see that she is covering her mouth to keep from bursting out laughing.

I start giggling. We lean on each other and laugh until I think I may wet my pants.

"Let's get a tantoo," says Jil when we finally calm down.

"I don't want a tattoo."

"Not a *tattoo*. A *tantoo*. You go to a tanning salon, to get a suntan, but you pick out a sticker that will cover part of your skin so you're left with a white patch that's shaped like a skull or a butterfly or something."

How does she know this stuff?

The next thing I know, I've ridden in a broken-down taxicab to a strip mall and I'm stretched out under a row of tanning lights. The tanning contraption is a long, clear plastic dome with a sort of cotlike bed under it, covered with a clean white sheet. I feel like the dead Snow White, except that I'm wearing tiny little plastic goggles to protect my eyes, and I'm naked. On my left butt cheek is a sticker shaped like a daisy.

Jil's in the next booth, so we talk through the walls.

"Whoa! This is so weird."

"Tingly."

"What if the timer doesn't shut this thing off?"

"We'll charbroil."

"Jil?"

"Yeah?"

"Don't you feel like the seven dwarves should be lined up around this thing?"

A hysterical whoop of laughter slices through our shared wall.

"I see Prince Charming," cries Jil.

"I see dead people," I answer. This is so much fun.

We go to Southern Lights for lunch—Jil's four-star recommendation. It's full of adults, talking loud and eating gourmet salads and sandwiches. I watch two stylish women at the next table, animating their conversation with exaggerated hand movements, acting like best friends, laughing.

That's me and Jil, I think, when we're fifty. The thought gives me a warm, happy feeling. Halfway through lunch, we sneak into the bathroom to look at our tantoos. The five-pointed star on Jil's left breast is showing up better than my butt-flower.

When the bill comes, I pull out the money that Mom gave me, but Jil won't let me pay. "It's the least I can do," says Jil.

"Well, okay . . . Thanks."

"Dez?"

"Yeah?"

"Thank *you*."

"Sure."

We sit there a minute, both sipping on our iced tea as if we're used to having fancy lunches every Wednesday.

"About tonight," says Jil, tugging on her left earlobe.

I take another sip of tea. I want to say, *No. Please. Not now. This is too much fun. Let's talk about that later.* With my index finger, I make a path through the cold beads of sweat that have formed on my glass.

"I've got a backup plan," says Jil.

I groan out loud.

She giggles. "No, really. Listen. The movie complex here is having a celebrate-summer, get-out-of-school special tonight. They're staying open all night and show-ing old movies. You know, kid-friendly ones—like *Star Wars*. It'll be one giant sleepover. Without the sleep part. If you're over twelve, you can get in without a parent. Dez. We can stay up all night."

"You're kidding?"

"Nope."

I'd been all set to tell her she was crazy again, and to talk her into coming home, but today's been so much fun. This freedom thing is cool. Besides, a whole night of movies sounds awesome. And my parents are trolls.

Jil is watching me expectantly.

"My mom's picking me up at four o'clock," I confess.

"I knew it," says Jil, slumping back in her chair. Abruptly, she sits up straight again, leans forward, her elbows on the table, her eyes dancing. "Call her," she says. "Call your mom. Tell her you need to stay a week."

"A week?" I ask. "The movie special lasts a week?"

"No, but we'll figure something else out tomorrow. Okay? Come on, Dez. When, in your whole life, will you ever be able to do this again?"

She has a point.

"Can I borrow your cell phone?" I ask.

She hands it to me, with my mom's number already punched in. All I have to do is push *Send*.

Jil's eyes are doing that amazing thing they do—radiating energy and enthusiasm enough to light a city.

For one brief second, I think, No—I have to keep Denver tomorrow. Then I remember. No, I don't. I'm not babysitting him tomorrow, or ever. Because Mom and Dad lied. They had so much faith in their one-and-only daughter that they never even cancelled day care. I smile back at Jil and push the button.

"Mom. Hi!" I say. "The piano class is awesome. Can I spend the rest of the week with Jil?"

Chapter Twenty

All these lies are making my stomach jerk. The excitement of a night with no parents has flooded my entire body with a million vibrating hummingbird wings. And the caffeine from my fourth glass of iced tea is making my heart *vroom* like somebody revving up a race car.

In a way, it feels fantastic. In another way, I want to throw up. Is this what it feels like to be drunk? I don't know. The only alcohol I ever tried was two forbidden swallows of the Lewises' Christmas eggnog. And that was two years ago.

"Jil," I say. "I think I've drunk too much tea."

"Me too," she answers gleefully. "Let's go shopping."

We take a cab to the mall.

"This is so cool." We race from one store to the next. "No curfew. No chores. No Denver to watch." As much as I hate how my parents dumped all over my Denver commitment, I'm feeling secretly happy to have my summer back. And I'm feeling totally ecstatic to have Jil back.

As far as my piano goes, I might as well have wished

for a planet.

We check out boys, try on jewelry, shoes, goofy hats—until our caffeine drops us both like two bowling balls. Jil crashes harder than I do.

"Dez," she says. "I'm dead." Her face is the color of a pair of Mom's sweatpants.

We find a seat at a small Formica-topped table in the food court and share an order of fries. She dumps the backpack she's been lugging around all day on the floor beside her chair. I'm guessing it has her things from Jane's house in it. Or at least the stuff she had time to grab before she took off.

The whole area smells like an overdose of world cookery—Mexican tacos, Chinese sweet-and-sour sauce, peppery Italian sausages, barbecue with hushpuppies, spicy egg rolls. All of it sizzling in too much overused peanut oil.

"Multicultural grease," I mumble, wiping lettuce and mustard off our table with a clean paper napkin. "Why can't people clean up their own mess?"

Jil shrugs and picks up her elbows so I can clean under them. "Tell me what happened," she says.

"About what?"

"About babysitting Denver."

I take my grungy napkin to the nearest trash receptacle, then sit back down with Jil and explain how Mom and Dad didn't believe I could do it. And how they never even cancelled day care. "So," I say, "it doesn't matter when I go home." I shove three French fries in my mouth, feeling yesterday's anger rush back over me. "I don't even care *if* I go home."

"Me, either," says Jil, double dipping her French fry into a tiny paper cup of ketchup.

I sit back in my chair and glare at her.

She pops the red-tipped fry into her mouth. "What?"

Suddenly, I'm so annoyed, but I don't want to spoil our day. How do I tell her that I think she's crazy? That I hate what her birth mom did to her, but what's that got to do with going home to her real mom and dad? The ones who, if you ask me, are the two best parents on earth!

"Jil," I say. "I know you're hurt. I totally get that, and I don't blame you. But why can't you go back to your real mom?"

Her eyes flash. "Because I hate her. I'll never go back."

"But why? She didn't do anything."

"Are you kidding? She accused me of stealing. Of introducing her daughter to a life of crime, of—"

"Jil," I interrupt. "I meant your *real* mom, not Jane."

"Jane *is* my real mom."

"Why does everybody keep saying that?" I hiss through clenched teeth. "*Real* isn't popping you out of the birth canal. It's raising you. Teaching you to tie your shoes. Holding your head when you barf. Knowing your favorite ice cream. Knowing *you*."

"Dez! Geez! Calm down. Who pushed *your* button?"

"You did!" I exclaim. "And stop sounding like my mom," I shout.

Jil gapes at me.

I wad up my napkin and scrub fiercely at the permanent ketchup stain on our tabletop, as if removing it can erase how stupid I just sounded.

"You know what I think?" says Jil. She's about to giggle.

I jerk my head up in disbelief. How can she be about to laugh when I just blew up at her?

"I think"—she circles a French fry gracefully in the air—"that we have parent issues." Jil's too tired for her eyes to radiate their usual megawatt energy, but the tips of them *are* crinkled up slightly, like her mouth. Radiating warmth. Friendship. Humor.

We both burst out laughing.

But just as suddenly, I stop. "Jil. Look. Don't pay any attention to me. I have no clue what's real. Obviously, Jane doesn't know you well enough to know that you would never swipe a necklace." I glance at her and feel the makings of a joke tugging at the corners of *my* mouth. "A soon-to-be-replaced street sign, maybe. But not a necklace."

Jil nods in grateful agreement.

"And *my* parents," I complain, "don't know *me* well enough to know that I'd keep Denver for a whole year if it meant I could get a piano. So," I say, tossing the mangled napkin onto our take-out tray, "maybe none of them is real."

Jil props one elbow on the table and rests her head

against her upright hand. "I wanted her to be," she says softly.

There's no hint of a joke anywhere. She just sounds sad.

"I know." I reach across the table and gently touch her arm.

"I won't go back there. Even if she begs me. But I don't want to go home, either. I'd have to tell Mom and Dad what she did, what Penny did, and then they'd never let me see either one of them again."

"Uh . . . Jil. I thought you didn't want to see either one of them again."

"I don't. But . . . but . . . I don't know . . . she's my mother!" Jil jerks her head up, then drops it back onto her hand. "Isn't she?" she almost whispers.

I want to help her. I want to say the perfect thing. But I don't have a clue what it is. Jil has found the people who look like her. They have her DNA—and her ear-pulling genes. And, in their own way, they love her. I think.

If I found a mom or dad who was that much like me, would I want to give him or her up forever?

"And, Dez. I'm sorry I made you lose your piano money. You can come play mine anytime you want."

"*Play* your piano?" I jokingly shove her arm so hard that it pops away from supporting her head. "Yesterday, you said I could *have* your piano!"

"Oh, yeah," she grins. "I did, didn't I? Well, you can come get it. Maybe Mom won't notice."

I picture Mrs. Lewis not detecting that there's a grand piano missing from her living room. I picture trying to put a grand piano in my den where it wouldn't fit, even if I removed all the trash and most of the furniture. Jil must have pictured the same thing, because we look up at each other and say, in perfect unison, "Parent issues."

After one more hour, even I am tired of the mall. How did Jil and Penny manage to spend whole days doing this? Did Penny swipe a necklace out of boredom? Who knows? But I can't wait for my whole night of movies.

I try not to think about what we'll do tomorrow. I especially try not to think what will happen to me if I get caught lying and living on the street like a homeless person. Well, not exactly a street—a movie theater.

The gang of kids in my library book *The Thief Lord* lived in a movie theater. An abandoned one—in Venice. That sounded incredibly cool when I read it, but now that I'm doing it, it's different. Nervous-and-scary different.

And my theater's not even deserted and cobwebby. No. It serves hot popcorn and thirty kinds of candy, but when tomorrow morning comes, then what?

At first, Mom freaked out wondering how I'd manage without a toothbrush, but I assured her that Greensboro does have drugstores. "Mom," I'd said. "Come on. I can buy one." So, she agreed to let me spend a few nights with Jil.

If you ask me, it's a trade-off for her guilt—for selling me out with Denver duty. But then Jil reminded me that Mom thinks I came to Greensboro to goof off and to go to piano camp. She has no clue that I came to save my best friend.

Whatever. It's exactly like Mom not to wonder what I'll do about clean clothes.

What *will* I do?

Chapter Twenty-one

About twenty minutes before five, we take a taxi to the movie theater. Our cab driver gives us the same curious look that the last one did. In Greensboro, North Carolina, thirteen-year-old girls ride around in cabs almost as often as they leap tall buildings with a single bound. It's just not normal.

We pay the special all-night price and rush inside—out of the heat. Immediately, I wish I had more clothes. Not clean ones. Warm ones. It's freezing in here!

I eye Jil's backpack. "Have you got a blanket in there?"

"Nope."

"A sweater?"

She shakes her head.

"What *do* you have?"

"I don't know . . . a toothbrush. Some makeup. Noxzema."

"*Peachy,*" I say, with all the sarcasm I can muster. "We can keep warm with eyeliner and globular chunks of zit cream."

Jil drops her bag to the floor, unzips it, and rummages

around inside. Finally her hand touches something that makes her smile. Triumphantly, she pulls out a pair of thick white tennis socks. "We can share," she announces proudly.

I will take her up on that.

We stroll over to a padded bench and plop down with the movie schedule—so we can decide which movies we want to see and in what order. Meanwhile, the place is filling up with kids—mostly hyper nine- and ten-year-olds with their parents. I figure older kids will show up later. We would've done that, too, but our current life situation gave us nothing better to choose from.

We thought about splurging on a fancy dinner somewhere, using Jil's credit card, but we've already eaten so many times today, we're just not up to it. Besides, I'm looking forward to a jumbo tub of buttered popcorn, a giant box of Junior Mints, an extra-extra-large Dr. Pepper, and some Sour Patch Kids for dessert.

The first movie that jumps off the page at me is *The Sisterhood of the Traveling Pants*. I'm pretty sure Jil notices it, too, because she's looking at me as if she's trying to pretend she doesn't see it, while trying, at the same time, to figure out whether I noticed it.

That's the great part about being best friends. You know what the other one is thinking.

For instance, I know she's wondering if that particular movie will make us happy or sad. Happy, because it's supposed to be a fun movie. Or sad, because every second of it will remind us of our Sisterhood of the Traveling Shirt—the one that never even saw its first swap because Penny still has the shirt.

"What the heck," says Jil, proving me right about reading her mind. "Let's go see it."

I borrow Jil's pen and carefully write *#1* beside the 5:00 showing of *Sisterhood*. Then we agree on *Charlie and the Chocolate Factory*, the Johnny Depp version, at 7:10. Movie #3, at 9:10, will be *Titanic*. Jil loves Leonardo DiCaprio, and I love blockbuster movies that make me cry. *So.* There you go.

I tap my head with the pen, and study the schedule. *Titanic* is over three hours long. "That takes us to 12:30. We need at least three more."

"*Planet of the Apes?*"

"Nah." I shake my head. "I've seen that a jillion times on TV."

"*Clueless?*"

"What's that about?"

"Some ultrapopular girls at a Beverly Hills high school." Jil flips back her hair dramatically and thrusts out her chest.

Which reminds me—we should probably check our tantoos again.

"One girl gets this brilliant idea to make over a nerd," Jil adds.

I glance up, seriously doubtful I want to spend two hours watching that.

"It's supposed to be good," Jil claims. "Honest. The plot got swiped right out of a Jane Austen novel."

"Jane Austen? The author? As in, *Pride and Prejudice*—the book I loved? *That* Jane Austen?"

"Yeah."

Neatly, I write #4 next to *Clueless*.

Jil reaches across me and points to *March of the Penguins*. "What's that about?"

"I think it's a documentary. In Antarctica. Rated G."

"Sounds boring," says Jil.

"Sounds cold." I shiver.

"*Pirates of the Caribbean*?"

I picture two more hours of Johnny Depp, plus Orlando Bloom. Perfect. I ink #5 beside it. "Okay. We need one more."

"*Jaws? Jurassic Park*?"

I tap the pen back and forth. "*Eeeny, meeny, miny, mo . . .*"

Jil leans on me. "Let's decide later."

"Good idea." I grab Jil's wrist and squeeze it. "Jil! Can you believe it? We're going to six movies! And stay up all night!"

Jil pumps her other fist. "Bring 'em on!"

The Sisterhood of the Traveling Pants does make us sad. And happy. We each pull on one of Jil's socks and joyfully declare ourselves the Overly Air-Conditioned Sisterhood of the Traveling Sock.

Charlie and the Chocolate Factory has dazzling candy-making scenes and is funny, but it keeps making us want to go back to the concession counter for more sugar.

"Dez," Jil asks as the final credits roll. "Was all that stuff about Willy Wonka's childhood in the book?"

"No." I think about the dog-eared paperback I read at least five times. "Definitely not."

"So, why do you think they added the part about him never being allowed to eat candy because his father was a dentist?"

I shrug. "Maybe they think you need a reason to be a candy inventor when you grow up."

"That's stupid."

"Yeah."

Titanic is one of those movies that makes me cry, even though I've already seen it twice. By the time it's over, I'm beat—as if I spent three hours treading water, all by myself, trying to keep that amazing ship from sinking.

When we straggle out, it's after midnight, and the crowd scene has totally changed. Parents are dragging their nine-year-olds to the exits. The kids are rubbing their red eyes, yawning, and arguing, "I did not fall asleep." High school kids fill the lobby, buying caffeine and candy, and killing time between movies.

I feel so grown up.

Then we realize we have to wait twenty-five minutes

for *Clueless* to begin, so we slip straight into *Pirates of the Caribbean* because it's just starting. I leave the numbers on our list the way they are, though, because if I try to change #4 to #5, it'll just make the whole thing messy.

I know. I'm a freak. I can't help it.

Two real loser guys follow us into *Pirates of the Caribbean*, then scrunch down in the seats directly behind us. They make gross kissing noises, laugh obnoxiously, and share with us every dirty word they know. If Mom were here, she'd tell them to wash their mouths out with soap.

The movie's great. Action-packed and funny. The only bad thing is that, while cannons boom on the screen in front of us, gross and stupid sound effects blast from the two creeps behind us. I think Jil or I should find an usher and complain, but when I turn to suggest it, she's sound asleep. Totally zonked from being up all night last night. No way I'm leaving her alone with Creep One and Creep Two.

When we file out of the movie, they stick to us like Band-Aids. In the hallway, we get our first good look at them. One guy has major zits and a slouch so curved I don't know why he doesn't slither to the floor. "Hey, babe!" he says with a goofball leer, tossing his car keys into the air and catching them. "How tall are you, anyway?"

Babe? Oh, please.

I'd love to pull out Jil's Noxzema and loan it to him, but memories of all those years of parent lectures about not talking to strangers—especially strangers with cars—make me shut up and ignore him.

In an artificial voice that reminds me of boots scraping on gravel, his creepy friend asks, "Who's your hottie friend?" Is he trying to sound sexy? He's dressed in an oversized football jersey and baggy shorts that droop almost to his ankles.

Jil and I make eye contact that confirms total agreement: Skip *Clueless*. Go directly to *March of the Penguins*.

They follow us anyway, but slouch-zit boy balks just inside the double doors and whines, "Ain't no chick worth this," and peels off to another movie.

Baggie-shorts boy groans, but decides to follow his buddy.

"Are we really going to watch this?" I ask Jil as we slip into our seats.

"You got a better idea?" Jil yawns. "I'm taking a nap."

She passes me a sock. I pull it over my right foot, then tuck my left foot up so that I'm sitting on it. Sleep sounds like a great idea. Can I sleep like this?

Jil's already curled up like a cat and looking as if she may snore any second, when the movie starts. A long line of tiny black somethings inches across an endless expanse of snow and ice.

I wish I had two socks.

But suddenly this movie is fascinating. Even Jil sits up. We watch the most amazing footage of penguins walking, penguins sliding, penguins falling in love. The photography blows me away.

But don't kid yourself. You do *not* want to be a penguin. Penguins walk seventy miles in insanely subzero temperatures, taking awkward, ice-clutching baby steps across slippery, frozen terrain. Sometimes they fall down.

Finally, they find this place where they mate. Eventually, each mom lays an egg, which she painstakingly passes to the father so he can hatch it while the moms walk seventy miles back to where they started. More baby steps. More falls. Just to get food to feed the soon-to-be-hatched chicks.

Which means—you guessed it—after they load up on a fish feast, they tiptoe another seventy miles back to the baby-hatching ground. Meanwhile, all the dads huddle up to survive the wild, blowing-like-crazy snowstorms. They practically freeze their feathers off trying to keep all those life-holding eggs from icing up and cracking.

And not a single one of them has eaten so much as a minnow for months.

Suddenly, I feel super guilty about the piles of food I've devoured in the last twelve hours. If I had any popcorn left at all, I'd give it to a penguin.

Jil and I leave the movie almost speechless.

"Wow."

"Yeah."

We wander into the ladies room for the fifth time. Maybe the sixth. I've lost count, but I know I've drunk a lot of Dr. Pepper. I go in and out of four stalls before I find one that hasn't run out of toilet paper. Used paper towels are spilling out of the trash cans. The air smells like you-know-what. But my tantoo is looking great.

Back in the lobby, we sit on a bench, trying to decide what to see next. I never thought I could see too many movies, but I'm getting a surround-sound headache in my eyeballs.

Jil elbows me in my ribs. I glance up and spot baggy-shorts boy and his zit-faced buddy purposefully slouch-walking in our direction, still showing off their cool and their car keys. Why would boys that old want to mess with thirteen-year-old girls?

"I can't deal with them," I whisper.

"Me, either."

"Bathroom," we echo each other, then split for the ladies room before Creep One and Creep Two ever know what happened.

Safely inside the restroom, we look at each other. "Now what?"

Jil answers me by hoisting her small self up onto the sink counter and leaning against the mirror, her size-5 feet dangling.

I moan. Then I grab a paper towel, wipe the counter clean of soap crud, and join her.

"Jil?"

"Yeah."

"How long do you think we'll have to sit in here?"

She shrugs. "I don't know."

"Those guys are scary. What if they follow us after we leave the building?"

"I don't know."

"Jil?"

"Yeah?"

"This is the second night in a row you've spent in a public bathroom."

"No kidding," she answers flatly.

For a long time, neither one of us says a word. I practice my fake piano, skillfully moving my fingers through the rotten-smelling air.

"What're you playing?" Jil asks.

" 'Für Elise.' " I run my fingers in a rapid little flourish, like a wave rolling smoothly, but swiftly, onto the shore.

"That's really beautiful," she says.

"Thanks." I play some more pretend music. Jil closes her eyes and grows silent. I wonder if she's listening, or has fallen asleep. Fake piano can only take me so far. My body is screaming that it wants to curl up somewhere soft, but my head is so jazzed up with caffeine and sugar, I doubt I could go to sleep—even if I had a bed.

I scrunch my butt around on the hard counter and try to get comfortable. The only thing I know for certain is that I want to go home.

"Dez?"

So. She's not asleep. "Yeah?"

"Do you think my mother would march seventy miles across an ice field to feed me?"

I hesitate. "Which mother?"

"Either."

Suddenly, I'm totally awake. My body and my head. What Jil is asking me is huge.

"What do you think?" I ask, stalling.

"I don't know. That's why I asked you."

I ponder it for a few seconds. Then I answer, "I think they both would."

"Really?" She bolts up straight, amazed. "You think Jane would do that for me?"

I carefully consider what to say next, and also what to make of the fact that she called her "Jane." But it's 4:30 in the morning and I'm a homeless kid in a bathroom that needs serious cleaning, so I decide to let my opinions pour out in whatever way they come to me.

"Jil," I say. "I think Jane *did* do that."

"What? Are you crazy? She never—"

"She gave you up. I bet that was a lot harder than walking seventy miles." I look over to see how she's reacting. She's staring at me.

"Jil," I continue, "she did it to *help* you. So that you'd be looked after, just right. Like the penguins."

Jil doesn't answer. She just has this zombielike blank stare.

"But your *real*, I mean, *adoptive* mom and dad have done just as much. More, actually," I add emphatically. "They've raised you. Every day. For thirteen years. And they'd definitely walk seventy miles to find you food. They'd walk a thousand miles. You know they would."

Still no answer.

Finally, Jil says, "Jane loves Penny more than me."

She's right. I know it. And she knows it, so there's no point in covering it up with a bunch of stupid lies.

"Yeah," I admit. "She probably does. But you know why, don't you?"

"No." Jil's voice cracks.

"Because she didn't just give birth to Penny. She raised her. Because she's been with her every day of her whole life. And I bet she's even more protective of her than normal. You know why?"

"Why?"

"Because she lost you, that's why. That makes the one-and-only daughter who lives with her even more special."

Jil is crying. I hear her, but I can't look at her. I've seen lots of sad stuff on movie screens tonight, but I can't make myself eyeball the real thing.

I listen to her choke and sniff and blow her nose. I hope she found a clean paper towel.

Finally, she says, "Do you remember the penguin whose baby died, and she was so upset she tried to steal someone else's?"

"Yeah."

"And all the other penguins pitched in and fought her off and wouldn't let her take it away?"

"Yeah." I'm nervous about where this is going.

"Well, that was about a fake mom trying to steal a baby from the real mom. But what's happening to me feels like the opposite. Jane's the real mom who some-how lost her own baby—me. But Mom and Dad are the adoptive parents who got to keep me. It's backward, like I'm a freak of nature or—" Jil can't finish because she's sobbing.

"Whoa!" I shout. "You are not a freak of anything. That's the stupidest thing I ever heard."

I slide off the counter and grab her and hug her. She is so tiny. She hugs me back, and says, "I know. You're right. I got carried away. Me. Jil. The drama queen." She hiccups and coughs out a nervous laugh. "I'm just so confused."

She slides out of my hug and slumps onto the floor. I stare at the filth she just sat down in, and I want to make her get up. But I don't. I sit down beside her. On the grimy floor. Where wet feet have tracked over the dirt and made everything muddy. The smell down here is even worse than it was higher up.

Neither one of us says anything for about a minute.

"Jil?"

"Yeah?"

"Do you really want to know what I think?"

"Yeah."

"I think there's a difference between being a parent, and being a mom or a dad."

"Huh?" She looks at me. Confused, but interested.

"Almost anybody can bring a baby into the world," I say. "But *parents* do more—like miss out on a great party because they can't find a good enough babysitter. Or they buy you your first bicycle instead of the TV they wanted for their bedroom. *Parents* make up stupid rules and worry about insane stuff—because they love you."

Jil tilts her head funny. She seems to be thinking, but her face is the color of a Red Hot.

Is she mad at me? I know I claimed I could read her mind, but that's just some of the time. Not all of the time.

Why doesn't she say something?

Finally, meekly, she says, "Yeah. You're right. You can be a mom—like Jane—and still not be a parent." Suddenly, her voice is firm. "But you know what else? I think being a parent is the part that makes them real."

Yes! I want to cheer. Instead, I say, "Does that mean we can go home?"

"Yeah," says Jil. "I'd like that."

I grin wider than the multiplex movie screen that all those penguins just Weeble-wobbled across. "Should we call Mom to come get us, or do you want to ask zit boy for a ride?"

Jil rolls her eyes, but she's not annoyed. She's happy.

Chapter Twenty-two

1 don't know how many germs there are on a bathroom floor, but I bet it's a staggering number. I hope I never find out.

Mom is going to drive over from Durham to pick us up in Greensboro—about an hour's drive. The bad thing is that we had to spend two hours in the bathroom before we even called her. I mean, I couldn't exactly call home at four something in the morning, could I?

The good news is that sometime between five and seven, Creep One and Creep Two apparently gave up and went home, because we never saw them again.

At seven A.M., I phoned Mom. I made up a lie about the piano camp teacher getting sick and calling everything off. Would she please come get us? Then I had to explain that Jil was going to cut her visit a little short, too. Mom said it all smelled fishy to her, and that she was up to her neck in alligators, but somehow, she'd rearrange her schedule and come get us anyway. Hopefully around ten o'clock.

Like I told Jil, that's the sort of things real parents do. So, even though Mom and I have nothing in common except blood and DNA, I'm grateful she's going to rescue us from our homelessness.

I'm also scared to death she and Dad will find out what we did.

After I hang up, we take what I sincerely hope is my last cab ride for a very long time. This driver is less suspicious than the others. Apparently he knows there was an all-night movie special, because he asks questions about our major film binge, then drops us at an IHOP, where Jil and I order waffles, eggs, bacon, and hash browns. We stare at the thick mounds of food, and eat as slowly as we possibly can, trying to pass enough time until we can reasonably show up at Jane's house. That's where Mom insisted on picking us up.

A person can only eat so much—or drink so many refills of water. Finally, the waitress asks us to please "vacate the table. People are waiting." Honest—that's the word she uses. *Vacate.* I think she's trying to sound polite, even though she's sick of bringing us water and ketchup and napkins and everything else we can think of to waste her time and ours. But we leave her a good tip to make up for it.

Outside, we hang around a while, killing more time, but mostly wanting to throw up all the stuff we've eaten in the last twenty-four hours. At nine-thirty, we walk the mile to Jane's house. The walking helps kill the feeling that I ate an elephant—with whipped cream and blueberry syrup.

Jane is super surprised to see us, but Jil makes up a

convincing story about my mom dropping us off while she's doing some pond business in Greensboro, and that she's going to pick us up again soon. Jil explains she wants to retrieve the rest of her stuff, but I also know she's secretly glad we had to go back there. It gives her a chance to leave Jane on happier terms.

They hug. They both even cry a little. Jil says she'll visit soon, and I think she will, but all of us know it won't be as often as before.

Jil and I sit on the porch steps and wait for Mom. We do *not* want her talking to Jane. The second we see her turn the corner, still a block away, we sprint for the curb. When we fling open the car doors, she says we look like something the cat dragged in.

So here we are, in Mom's muddy Subaru, and you know what? It almost looks good to me—except for the crumpled take-out bag and the wadded-up Egg McMuffin wrappers that are covering the floor where my feet want to be.

We're cruising down the highway now. Mom asking about piano camp. Jil making up lies. Me dying to take a shower.

Finally, Mom says, "Dez. Why is it that every time I ask you a question, Jil answers it?"

A nervous little half laugh pops out of me. "Oh, Mom. You know Jil."

"I know you," she answers suspiciously.

"What's that supposed to mean?" I ask, totally offended.

I'm a good kid! Doesn't she know that? I don't lie! Well, hardly ever. At least, not until lately.

"Honestly, Dez," she says, her shoulders sinking as she blows out a giant sigh. "Your dad and I are a little disappointed."

"With what?"

"With you."

"Fine." I slump down in my seat and cross my arms. Half of me is embarrassed that Jil's in the backseat listening, but the other half is thrilled that she's hearing the mess she got me into.

"I mean, really. What would you think?" Mom continues. "First you want a piano. So much that you promise to babysit Denver. A day later, you don't want a piano."

"I never—"

"Let me finish. You just *had* to go to piano day camp— the greatest experience since sliced bread. The next day, you don't want that, either."

"I told you, it got canceled."

Mom turns and levels a parent look at me, the one that you have to master in order to graduate from parent school—birth or adoptive. The one that says, *Don't lie to me, young lady.*

And I don't want to lie. I hate lying. But what can I say without breaking my promise to Jil? Or telling her that I spent the night in a bathroom? So I don't say anything.

When Mom and I drop Jil off, she can't even look at me. I realize that I have no clue what she's going to tell her parents. And I don't want to know, either. Because it'll mean more lies for me to remember.

A split second before she shuts the car door, she reaches into the front seat and stuffs something soft into my hand.

"Bye, Mrs. Carter! Thank you so much for the ride. Bye, Dez!"

I look down in my hand. I'm holding one slightly soiled white tennis sock.

Five minutes later, I'm in the shower. In my own house. *Yes!* Letting hot water stream over every inch of me, carrying off all the germs that were multiplying like rabbits on that bathroom floor. I get barfy just thinking about it. My bar of soap is half the size I started with. If I have to, I'll rub all my skin off, just to get rid of the bacteria. I wish I could scrub off the dishonesty.

I think about Jil and her family, and how happy I am that she's home. Isn't that worth a few lies?

I squeeze lemon-scented shampoo into my hands and breathe in deeply, flooding my nose and my whole body with the fresh, wonderful smell. Slowly, I lather it up, then massage it into my scalp with my fingertips.

Closing my eyes, I relax and think, my parents are real, too. In every way. Biologically. Practically. Annoyingly. They'd walk seventy miles in the snow to bring me food. Just like Jil's parents would. So why should I care if what they show up with is Cheez Whiz instead of real cheddar? Or that they won't wash the dirty dishes?

I admit, spending a night on the wet floor of a public bathroom has made me a little bit less critical of my house, but still . . .

I rinse off the shampoo, dry off with a reasonably clean towel, and climb into bed. So what if it's not even noon yet? Has any bed ever felt this good? I think not.

I curl up and wonder what I'll do all summer, now that there will be no piano. No babysitting job.

I wish I'd asked Mr. Trimble for a list of summer book suggestions. Then I could read tales with happy endings. Stories where the well-meaning girl, the one who sacrifices everything to help her friend, gets the piano.

In real life, I know that just doesn't happen. Well, maybe it happens to people like Jil. But never to me. Because I know my parents. We will never own a piano.

My birthday is in two weeks. I'll be lucky if they give me a pencil.

Chapter Twenty-three

"**S**urprise!"

A dozen people leap from behind doors and chairs and sofas as I stroll into my den. They're dressed funny, and they're all singing "Happy Birthday." Loud, laughing, and completely off-key. Dad seems to be whistling the melody into a long wooden flute.

Jil, Mom, Dad, Denver, the Lewises, plus a few of my friends from school. I spot Samantha and Michelle. Even Graham is here. Is he wearing a tunic? Why does Dad have on a chain-link fence instead of a shirt?

I'm excited. I'm horrified.

Don't get me wrong. A surprise party is an awesome thing. But, at *my* house? With *my* parents in charge? *That* is scary. It's the Tater T-shirts element multiplied by the Cheez Whiz factor. Plus, fourteen years of successfully keeping friends from seeing the inside of my house—straight down the drain.

Jil flies across the room and throws her arms around me. Wait a minute. Isn't she grounded? For life?

Last week, when she confessed to her parents the real reason she bailed on her Mom-2 visit, her story got so tangled that, before she knew it, the whole truth spilled out. Stuff like sleeping on a toilet at Target. Even the Lewises couldn't ignore that many lies and that much dumbness.

But here she is, wearing a pointy princess hat with a peach-colored silk scarf floating down from its peak, and she's shouting, "Surprise! Happy Birthday!"

She squeezes me in a quick hug and whispers, "They freed me—just for tonight," then pushes me into the kitchen.

Everyone follows.

Mom and Dad stare at me, almost shyly. Expectantly.

A long fold-out Formica table has been set up in the middle of the room. Soup bowls filled with something smelly and lumpy are scattered across the top. Next to them sit thick slabs of fossilized bread covered with overcooked chicken drumsticks and slathered with . . . with . . . I don't know what. Food that is green and gray and mushy and gross.

"It's a medieval feast!" exclaims Dad, flourishing his flute to include the whole room.

Oh. That explains the shirt. It's supposed to be chain mail—the part that goes under the armor.

"Have some clarrey," says Mom, grinning and offering me a heavy mug filled with golden liquid. She's wearing a stained, baggy, no-waist dress that hangs to her ankles. I'm guessing she's some kind of medieval scullery maid, but she looks about the same to me.

"Clarrey?" I ask.

"It's wine," says Graham, grinning and throwing down a huge swig, then wiping his mouth on his sleeve. Next, he actually tries to pinch Michelle, who shrieks and blushes. I guess that means he's getting totally into the character that matches his costume—tunic-wearing barbarian. More importantly, I guess it means he's getting over Jil.

But my brain is too busy to think about that. It's still trying to process Mom's handing me an alcoholic beverage. Parents can be clueless, but no way did mine confuse my fourteenth birthday with my twenty-first. I stare at the mug. "Wine?"

"Clarrey," explains Dad. "Or more accurately, *vinum claratum*. It comes from the Latin, meaning 'clarified wine.' In the twenty-first century, we call it claret."

"You're serving wine? To minors?" I'm having trouble making sense of any of this. Especially the wine part.

"Of course not," says Dad. "It's apple juice. But I made it from a medieval recipe that calls for mulling spices and wine. Obviously," he pauses and winks at me, "I omitted the wine. Instead, I substituted apple juice, then added honey, cinnamon, cardamom, galingale—"

"Galin . . . what?"

"*Galingale*—it's a spice. Made from a plant in the sedge family. With red flowers and aromatic roots. The Latin name, *Cyperus longus*—"

"Dad!"

"Oh. Sorry." He bows apologetically to everyone in the room for accidentally inflicting a history/botany/Latin lesson on us. But he still can't stop himself from adding, "I substituted ginger for the galingale. Food Lion hasn't carried galingale for centuries."

Everyone laughs like Robin Hood's band of merry men. They're all having a blast.

I'm mortified.

"Thanks, Dad. Mom. Everybody." I force a smile. "This is so fun."

"Are you really surprised?" asks Samantha.

"Utterly," I answer. It's the most honest thing I've said in days.

"Let's eat!" shouts Mom, slapping Mr. Lewis on his back.

I want to die.

We all sit around the table in folding chairs and slurp down the lumpy liquid that's in the bowls. Apparently it's cabbage soup with who-knows-what old-English ingredients simmered in.

The chicken-and-bread stack is called a trencher. That, as Dad couldn't wait to tell me, is a chunk of stale bread with roasted chicken, eggs, asparagus, potatoes, and miscellaneous yuck heaped on top. Apparently, before plates were invented, people just slopped everything in a gross pile on top of very old bread.

Mr. Lewis picks up the whole thing and chomps into it as if he's been eating like a pig all his life. Denver is rolling meatballs to Jil. She is actually rolling them back, but the ones he doesn't catch are hitting the floor.

"Dogs and vermin generally cleaned up the spillage,"

says Dad, clearly disappointed that we don't have any rats.

I look around at our messy, dirty house and decide that I wouldn't be a bit surprised if one or two showed up.

That's when I realize that this party is the perfect cover-up for my parents' bad habits. I bet all the guests think that my parents went out of their way to make it dirty and messy especially for the party.

I almost laugh out loud.

Elegant Mrs. Lewis, dressed in a flowing blue brocade robe, gnaws on the last bite of her chicken, then tosses the bone over her shoulder and onto the floor.

As Mom would say, *that* brings the house down. Everyone laughs until we practically fall out of our chairs. Actually, Graham *does* fall out of his chair. Not to be outdone, Denver tries to do a headstand in his and falls over backward, crying but, miraculously, unhurt.

From that point on, I have fun.

There are only two disappointments. The first is the cake, which isn't a cake at all, but a bunch of authentic medieval poached pears with fourteen very unmedieval birthday candles pushed into them. The pears taste great, but still . . . a pear is not a birthday cake. A pear is fruit.

The second disappointment is my present from Mom and Dad. It isn't a piano. Even when you know, 100 percent, that you're not getting something, you still hope.

What I get instead is a new winter coat. Mom had noticed, at the Lewises' Christmas party, that maybe I needed a dressier coat. I definitely give her major points for noticing something so un-Momlike, but excuse me, it's June. How excited can I get about a wool coat?

Finally, as everyone leaves, Jil pulls me aside and whispers, "Can you believe it?"

I say, "No. I really can't," shaking my head in disbelief, then adding, "But who would have thought—this was really fun, wasn't it?"

Suddenly, I remember that she's grounded. And I'm not. My shoulders sink. Sooner or later, I ought to tell *my* parents what happened, too. But I promised Jil I wouldn't.

"I'm sorry you're in so much trouble," I say. Then, I straighten myself up and exclaim, "But I'm so glad they let you come tonight!"

"Me, too!" shrieks Jil. Then she gets a serious look on her face, and says, "Dez, I know I can never, ever repay you for everything you did for me, but I tried."

"You tried?" I ask.

"Yeah. I tried to make it up to you."

"Thanks. What'd you do? Help with the party?"

"Nope."

"Tell Mom I needed a coat?"

"Nope."

"Jil. What did you do?"

"You'll see."

"*Jil!*"

"Bye." She waves casually on her way out the door. Her eyes are dancing again. "Happy Birthday!"

Chapter Twenty-Four

Mom and Dad have piled all the dirty dishes in the sink—a leaning tower of soup bowls. At least there aren't any dinner plates. Just a garbage disposal stuffed full of stale bread chunks and a trash can full of chicken bones. I know I should help load the dishwasher, but I hate stacked bowls—the food gets smeared all over the bottoms. Why do people do that?

Mom has collapsed onto the sofa, and Dad is lying back in his recliner, looking even paler than usual but satisfied. Denver is already in his bed, fast asleep.

Quietly, with his eyes closed, Dad whispers, "'*And pomp, and feast, and revelry, with mask, and antique pageantry, such sights as youthful poets dream, on summer eves by haunted stream.*'" He opens one eye, smiles at me, and says, "John Milton."

I smile back and say, "'*Goodnight room, goodnight moon*'—Margaret Wise Brown."

I slip away to my room to put away my birthday presents. I can't wait to use the label maker that Jil gave me. That has got to be the best present anyone's ever heard of.

But what did Jil mean? What did she do to help me? Help me with what?

"Dez," calls Mom. "Can you come here a minute?"

I carefully slide the *Beginner's Book of Piano Classics* that the Lewises gave me into my desk drawer. I'll need to redraw my fake piano keyboard so I can use it. Heaving a huge sigh, I join Mom and Dad in the den.

"Thanks again for the party," I say.

"You're welcome, Dez. Sit down, please." Dad's voice is weird. Tense? Tired? I can't tell.

I perch on the edge of our worn-out plaid armchair and wait.

"Tomorrow, we're having a piano delivered," says Dad.

"*What!*" I leap out of my chair. "For me? A piano for me? You're kidding, right?" I look from Mom to Dad, then back to Mom. They're smiling.

"Really? You mean it?" I sit back down. Frozen. Afraid to believe them.

"We thought it was just a phase. But we were wrong." Mom leans forward and takes my hand.

"Apparently you've been doing some growing up when we weren't watching," Dad adds.

"I have?"

"That was quite a sacrifice you made," says Dad.

"It was?"

"Jil told us everything," explains Mom.

"Everything?"

"Honey," says Mom. "You sound like an echo." She

squeezes my hand. "We're very proud that you were willing to give up something so important for a friend in need."

I'm speechless.

"And Jil told us you practically play air piano in your sleep."

Did she tell them I played air piano in a bathroom at four A.M.?

"So, we're going to let you try out a piano. We rented a small upright, with an option to buy."

"What's that mean?"

"It means that if you practice, and continue to play, we can buy the piano, and all the rental money we've paid will count toward the purchase price."

I jump up and hug Mom. I fly across the room to Dad, who, in order to brace himself better this time for one of my tackle hugs, has quickly popped his recliner into the up position.

"Mrs. Lewis gave us the name of a real piano teacher she thinks you'll like. She said your talent needs fostering."

"Oh, Mom. Dad. Thank you. You won't be sorry." I'm jumping up and down, not looking mature at all, but I don't care. "I'll practice every day. I'll help pay for my lessons. I'll get a job. I'll keep Denver. I'll—"

"Dez," says Dad, holding up his hand. "Enough. First, you have to pay Jil's parents back the money you charged on their credit card."

"What on earth were you thinking?" exclaims Mom. Dad nods in total agreement.

"Start by helping out around the house while you're grounded. Then you'll need a real job. Your mother will pay you to ride along with her and take field notes for her pond research."

I sit back down with a *whump*. "I'm grounded?"

"Well, let's see," says Mom. She holds up all the fingers on her right hand and starts counting. "You lied about where you were going. You lied about what you were doing. You lied about—"

"But it was all for Jil. I hated doing that. You said—"

"That we were proud of you," Dad finishes my sentence. "And we were. We are. You sacrificed your credibility about wanting a piano, just to help Jil. And she needed you, Dez. You helped her with a dangerously difficult problem—understanding who her parents are." Dad smiles and lowers his chair back into the recline position. "You should have heard all the complimentary things she said about your good sense . . . your intelligent thinking."

"But," says Mom, "you lied like a rug. And running around all night on your own . . ." She shakes her head in a series of disbelieving little jerks. "You could have been harmed. Anything could've happened. We're absolutely furious about that part!"

My head's spinning. Jil told them everything—I did a good thing. Jil told them everything—I did a bad thing.

Jil told them the truth about things she didn't want anyone to know—ever. I don't have to keep her secret
anymore. I'm getting a piano. I have talent that needs
fostering. I'm intelligent. So, how come I understand Jil's
parents and not my own? Or do I? They're messy—I'm
neat. They'd walk seventy miles in a blizzard for me.
I'm grounded. I may be spending half my summer in
a hard hat. With spotted newts. And my mother. Will
that be interesting? Or muddy. It's all way too much to
sort out.

For now, I think I'll just concentrate on one thing at a
time. First things first, as Mom would say.

I press three fingers of my left hand—pinky, middle
finger, thumb—carefully into the air in front of my left
elbow. A perfect chord. The key of C. The fingers on
my right hand dance lightly across the empty space to my
right. A brisk melody, playful and easy. My posture is
centered, elbows slightly out, wrists flat. And my fingers
never leave the keys.